William Shakespeare's All's Well that Ends Well: A Retelling in Prose

David Bruce

Published by David Bruce, 2022.

This is a work of fiction. Similarities to real people, places, or events are entirely coincidental.

WILLIAM SHAKESPEARE'S ALL'S WELL THAT ENDS WELL: A RETELLING IN PROSE

First edition. July 22, 2022.

Copyright © 2022 David Bruce.

ISBN: 979-8201468545

Written by David Bruce.

Table of Contents

Dedication

Dedicated to Carl Eugene Bruce and Josephine Saturday Bruce

My father, Carl Eugene Bruce, died on 24 October 2013. He used to work for Ohio Power, and at one time, his job was to shut off the electricity of people who had not paid their bills. He sometimes would find a home with an impoverished mother and some children. Instead of shutting off their electricity, he would tell the mother that she needed to pay her bill or soon her electricity would be shut off. He would write on a form that no one was home when he stopped by because if no one was home he did not have to shut off their electricity.

The best good deed that anyone ever did for my father occurred after a storm that knocked down many power lines. He and other linemen worked long hours and got wet and cold. Their feet were freezing because water got into their boots and soaked their socks. Fortunately, a kind woman gave my father and the other linemen dry socks to wear.

My mother, Josephine Saturday Bruce, died on 14 June 2003. She used to work at a store that sold clothing. One day, an impoverished mother with a baby clothed in rags walked into the store and started shoplifting in an interesting way: The mother took the rags off her baby and dressed the infant in new clothing. My mother knew that this mother could not afford to buy the clothing, but she helped the mother dress her baby and then she watched as the mother walked out of the store without paying.

***

The doing of good deeds is important. As a free person, you can choose to live your life as a good person or as a bad person. To be a good person, do good deeds. To be a bad person, do bad deeds. If you do good deeds, you will become good. If you do bad deeds, you will become bad. To become the person you want to be, act as if you already are that kind of person. Each of us chooses what kind of person we will become. To become a good person, do the things a good person does. To become a bad person, do the things a bad person does. The opportunity to take action to become the kind of person you want to be is yours.

Human beings have free will. According to the Babylonian Niddah 16b, whenever a baby is to be conceived, the Lailah (angel in charge of contraception) takes the drop of semen that will result in the conception and asks God, "Sovereign of the Universe, what is going to be the fate of this drop? Will it develop into a robust or into a weak person? An intelligent or a stupid person? A wealthy or a poor person?" The Lailah asks all these questions, but it does not ask, "Will it develop into a righteous or a wicked person?" The answer to that question lies in the decisions to be freely made by the human being that is the result of the conception.

A Buddhist monk visiting a class wrote this on the chalkboard: "EVERYONE WANTS TO SAVE THE WORLD, BUT NO ONE WANTS TO HELP MOM DO THE DISHES." The students laughed, but the monk then said, "Statistically, it's highly unlikely that any of you will ever have the opportunity to run into a burning orphanage and rescue an infant. But, in the smallest gesture of kindness — a warm smile, holding the door for the person behind you, shoveling the driveway of the elderly person next door — you have committed an act of immeasurable profundity, because to each of us, our life is our universe."

In her book titled *I Have Chosen to Stay and Fight*, comedian Margaret Cho writes, "I believe that we get complimentary snack-size portions of the afterlife, and we all receive them in a different way." For Ms. Cho, many of her snack-size portions of the afterlife come in hip hop music. Other people get different snack-size portions of the afterlife, and we all must be on the lookout for them when they come our way. And perhaps doing good deeds and experiencing good deeds are snack-size portions of the afterlife.

The Zen master Gisan was taking a bath. The water was too hot, so he asked a student to add some cold water to the bath. The student brought a bucket of cold water, added some cold water to the bath, and then threw the rest of the water on a rocky path. Gisan scolded the student: "Everything can be used. Why did you waste the rest of the water by pouring it on the path? There are some plants nearby which could have used the water. What right do you have to waste even a drop of water?" The student became enlightened and changed his name to Tekisui, which means "Drop of Water."

Educate Yourself
Read Like A Wolf Eats
Be Excellent to Each Other
Books Then, Books Now, Books Forever

***

In this retelling, as in all my retellings, I have tried to make the work of literature accessible to modern readers who may lack some of the knowledge about mythology, religion, and history that the literary work's contemporary audience had.

Do you know a language other than English? If you do, I give you permission to translate this book, copyright your translation, publish or self-publish it, and keep all the royalties for yourself. (Do give me credit, of course, for the original retelling.)

I would like to see my retellings of classic literature used in schools, so I give permission to the country of Finland (and all other countries) to give copies of this book to all students forever. I also give permission to the state of Texas (and all other states) to give copies of this book to all students forever. I also give permission to all teachers to give copies of this book to all students forever.

Teachers need not actually teach my retellings. Teachers are welcome to give students copies of my eBooks as background material. For example, if they are teaching Homer's *Iliad* and *Odyssey*, teachers are welcome to give students copies of my *Virgil's* Aeneid: *A Retelling in Prose* and tell students, "Here's another ancient epic you may want to read in your spare time."

CAST OF CHARACTERS

Male Characters

King of France
Duke of Florence
Bertram, Count of Rousillon
Lafeu, an old Lord
Parolles, a follower of Bertram
Rinaldo, a Steward
Lavache, a Professional Fool

Female Characters

Countess of Rousillon, Mother to Bertram
Helena, daughter to Gerard de Narbon, a famous physician, six months dead at the beginning of the play. She is sometimes called Helen.
An old Widow of Florence
Diana, daughter to the Widow
Mariana, neighbor and friend to the Widow

Minor Characters

Several young French Lords, serving with Bertram in the Florentine wars
Lords attending on the King, Officers, Soldiers, etc.

Scene

Partly in France and partly in Tuscany
Rousillon is in the south of France

CHAPTER 1

— 1.1 —

A number of people spoke together in the palace of Bertram, the Count of Rousillon: Bertram; his mother, the Countess of Rousillon; Helena, her ward; and Lafeu, an elderly lord.

The Countess said, "In delivering my son from me, I bury a second husband."

She was delivering her son to the King of France. Her husband, who was her son's father, had died, and her son had become the King of France's ward. Now her son, Bertram, was going to the court of the King of France. The Countess was saying that by allowing her son to go to the King's court, her grief at being separated from her son was such that it was like she was burying a second husband.

Bertram said to her, "And I in going, madam, weep anew over my father's death, but I must pay heed to his majesty's command, whose ward I am now and to whom I am evermore in subjection."

Lafeu said, "You shall find in the King a husband, aka a protector, madam; you, Bertram, sir, shall find in the King a father. This King who is to all men and at all times good must of necessity maintain his virtue in his dealings with you. Your worthiness is such that it would stir virtue up where it was lacking rather than lack virtue where there is such abundance."

"What hope is there of his majesty's health being restored?" the Countess asked.

"He has abandoned his physicians, madam," Lafeu said. "Under their medical practices he has made his life miserable with hope; he has stayed alive and suffered pain in the hope of finding a cure, but now he finds no advantage in the process except only the losing of hope by time. Time passed, and now he has lost all hope of recovering his health."

The Countess said, "This young gentlewoman, Helena, had a father — oh, that word 'had'! How sad a passage, both a turn of phrase and a way to the next life, it is! — whose skill as a physician was almost as great as his honesty. Had his skill stretched as far as his honesty, it would have made nature immortal, and the god of death would have lots of time for play because of lack of work. I wish, for the King's sake, her father the physician was still living! I think it would be the death of the King's disease."

"What is the name of the man you speak of, madam?" Lafeu asked.

"He was famous, sir, in his profession, and it was his great right to be so: Gerard de Narbon," the Countess replied.

"He was excellent indeed, madam," Lafeu said. "The King very recently spoke of him admiringly and mournfully. Her father the physician was skillful enough to be alive forever, if knowledge could be set up against human mortality."

"What is it, my good lord, the King languishes of?" Bertram asked.

"A fistula, my lord," Lafeu replied.

A fistula is an ulcerous sore.

"I had not heard about it before," Bertram said.

"I wish that it were not widely known," Lafeu replied.

He then asked the Countess, "Was this gentlewoman here — Helena — the daughter of Gerard de Narbon?"

The Countess replied, "She was his sole child, my lord, and she is bequeathed to my guardianship — she is now my ward. I have high hopes for her. Her education and upbringing promise good things, as do the mental qualities she inherited. These things make fair gifts fairer; for where an unclean character carries virtuous qualities, there commendations go with pity. They are virtues and traitors, too."

Think of thieves. We prefer that thieves be stupid so that they are easily caught. We do not want thieves to have good qualities such as bravery and intelligence because the good qualities make the thieves more competent and successful at committing evil. Instead, we prefer that people of good character have good qualities.

The Countess continued, "Helena's good qualities are the better for their innocence; she was born with a clean mind and she works hard to achieve a good character."

"Your commendations of her, madam, have caused her to cry tears," Lafeu said.

"Salty tears are the best brine a maiden can preserve her praise in," the Countess said. "The memory of her father never approaches her heart without the cruelty of her sorrows taking all vivacity from her cheeks.

"No more of this, Helena; please, no more, lest it be thought you affect — display — a sorrow rather than have ...."

The Countess' own grief rose in her and she did not finish her sentence.

Helena thought, *I do affect a sorrow indeed, but I have it, too. I show my sorrow in my face, but I feel my sorrow in my mind, too.*

Lafeu said, "Moderate lamentation is the right of the dead; excessive grief is the enemy to the living."

The Countess said, "If the living is an enemy to the grief, the excess makes it soon mortal."

The Countess agreed with Lafeu; the living must handle grief the correct way. In the *Iliad*, Achilles does not handle his grief at the death of his friend Patroclus the right way; his grief is excessive. Odysseus explains the right way to mourn for the dead: A loved one dies, we mourn for a while, and then we return to living our life. Mourning a dead person excessively can destroy a living person.

Bertram changed the subject by saying, "Madam, I desire your holy wishes."

Lafeu asked, "How are we to understand that?"

He was pointing out that Bertram was rude to change the subject so abruptly. They were giving advice to Helena about how to handle grief, advice that would also help the Countess, and Bertram ought not to change the subject so abruptly.

The Countess, however, blessed her son: "Be you blest, Bertram, and may you succeed your father in manners and other acquired characteristics, as you do in his shape and appearance! May your nobility and virtue contend for empire in you, and may your acquired goodness share with your inherited qualities!

"Love all, trust a few, do wrong to none. Be capable and prepared to deal with your enemy rather in power than in use — if you are powerful enough to resist your enemy, your enemy will refrain from attacking you.

"Protect and value your friend's life as you protect and value your own life.

"Be rebuked for silence, but never be criticized for speech. Accept whatever other gifts Heaven is willing to give you as a result of your own efforts and my prayers — may these Heavenly gifts descend upon your head!

"Farewell."

She then said to Lafeu, "My lord, my son is an unseasoned and inexperienced courtier. My good lord, advise him."

Lafeu replied, "Bertram cannot lack the best advice — the best people shall accompany his love."

Lafeu was aware that good companions would advise their friend well.

"May Heaven bless him!" the Countess said. "Farewell, Bertram."

She exited.

Bertram said to Helena, "May the best wishes that can be forged in your thoughts be servants to you! Be comforting to my mother, your mistress, and make much of her. Serve her well."

"Farewell, pretty lady," Lafeu said to Helena. "You must live up to the good reputation of your father."

Bertram and Lafeu exited.

Alone, Helena said to herself, "Oh, I wish that were all I had to do! I don't think about my father; and these great tears on my face now would grace his memory more than those I shed for him when he died. What was he like? I have forgotten him. My imagination carries no one's face in it but Bertram's.

"I am undone and ruined. There is no life for me, none, if Bertram is away from me. It is the same as if I were to love a bright particular star and think to wed it — Bertram is so above me in social rank. I must be comforted in his bright radiance and parallel light, not in his sphere. The sphere I am in is lower than the sphere that Bertram is in. I can see the light that comes from his sphere, but I can never reach the sphere that he is in."

Helena was referring to the astronomical beliefs of her society. The Earth was thought to be the center of the universe, and the planets and stars were located in spheres above and surrounding the Earth. The planets and stars stayed in their own spheres and did not travel in between spheres.

Helena continued speaking to herself, "The ambition in my love thus plagues itself: I want to marry above my station. The hind — the female deer — that would be mated by the lion must die for love.

"It was pretty pleasure, although it was also a plague, to see Bertram every hour, to sit and draw his arched brows, his hawk-like eye, his curls, on the canvas of my heart — a heart too capable of taking in and perceiving every line and trick of his sweet appearance.

"But now he's gone, and my idolatrous fancy must sanctify his relics."

She heard a noise, looked up, and said, "Who is coming here?"

Parolles entered the room. His name suggested the French word *"paroles,"* which means "words." Parolles was boastful and full of words and exaggerated his courage, of which he had little or none.

Helena recognized him and said to herself, "He is one who goes with and accompanies Bertram. I treat this man as a friend for Bertram's sake, and yet I know that he is a notorious liar. I think that he is in a great way a fool, and entirely a coward; yet these fixed evils of foolishness and cowardice are so suitably lodged in him that they find acceptance and take precedence when virtue's steely bones look bleak in the cold wind."

This man, Parolles, was a bad man, but he was so well suited to be a bad man and so ill suited to be a good man that people accepted his badness. Some scoundrels are accepted by others who know that they are scoundrels. Parolles, however, attempted to keep his badness secret, although in time people often found out about his true character.

Helena continued talking to herself, "It is true that very often we see cold wisdom waiting on superfluous folly."

A wise servant can serve a foolish master. An ill-dressed, and therefore cold, servant, can serve an extravagant and overdressed master.

Parolles greeted Helena, "May God save you, fair Queen!"

"And may God save you, King!" Helena replied.

"I am no King," Parolles said.

"And I am no Queen," Helen replied.

"Are you meditating on virginity?"

"Yes," Helena replied.

She was in fact a virgin, and she wanted to be married to Bertram, something that was very unlikely to happen. How could she, a virgin, pursue marriage with a man while still retaining her modesty?

She said to Parolles, "You have some tinge of a soldier in you. Let me ask you a question. Man is the enemy to female virginity; how may we women *barricado* — defend with barricades — our virginity against him?"

"Keep him out," Parolles replied.

"But he assails our virginity; and our virginity, although valiant, is yet weak in its defense. Unfold to us women some warlike resistance we can use to defend our virginity," Helena said.

"There is none," Parolles said. "Man, sitting down before you, will undermine you and dig deep and blow you up."

Parolles was using military terminology. "To sit down before" meant "to besiege." "To undermine" meant "to dig deep and lay a mine" and "to blow you up" meant "to cause an explosion that will blow you up."

He was also punning. The man's penis would dig deep in a metaphorical mine and plant a seed that would cause the woman's belly to blow up with pregnancy.

"Bless our poor virginity from underminers and blowers up!" Helena said. "Is there no military policy or trick in which virgins might blow up men?"

Parolles replied, "Virginity being blown down, man will all the more quickly be blown up."

Once a virgin is successfully blown down, perhaps on a bed, the man's penis will quickly be blown up — it will become erect.

He continued, "By Mother Mary, in blowing him down again, with the breach yourselves made, you lose your city."

The way to blow a man down again is to cause him to orgasm. This is something that a woman can do by making use of the breach — opening — in her. Once the man orgasms, his penis will stop being erect. But by that time, what is being defended — virginity — has been lost.

He continued, "It is not politic in the commonwealth of nature to preserve virginity. Loss of virginity is rational increase and there was never a virgin begotten until virginity was first lost."

Loss of virginity leads to rational increase — a woman loses her virginity and then gives birth to a rational creature. The only way for a virgin to be born is for a virgin — the future mother — to lose her virginity.

He continued, "That substance which you are made of is metal and mettle — stuff and disposition — used to make new virgins. You are a woman, and you were born to make new virgins. Virginity by being once lost may be ten times found; once you lose your virginity, you can give birth to ten virgin children. If you keep forever your virginity, you lose forever the ability to make new virgins. Virginity is too cold a companion; away with it!"

"I will stand for it a little, although therefore I die a virgin," Helena said.

Her words were ambiguous. The first and most obvious meaning was that she would continue to be a virgin for a while even though it might mean that she would die while she was still a virgin. In this society, however, "a stand" is "an erection," and "to die" means "to have an orgasm." Therefore, another meaning of what she had said was this: "I will stand, aka submit to, an erection for a while, although by doing that I will have an orgasm and my virginity will come to an end."

Parolles said, "There's little that can be said in the defense of virginity; virginity is against the rule of nature. To speak in favor of virginity is to accuse your mother, who ceased to be a virgin, and that is most indubitably disrespect to your mother.

"He who hangs himself is a virgin in this respect: virginity murders itself."

A person who commits suicide and a virgin are similar in that a suicide and a virgin are denying life to any future progeny. Therefore, their genes will not be continued in their progeny who are never born.

He continued, "The suicides and the virgins should be buried in highways in unsanctified ground, as desperate offenders and offendresses against nature. Virginity breeds mites, much like a cheese does. Both breed their own destruction. The virgin leaves behind no progeny and so ensures the death of the virgin's line. The cheese becomes a breeding place for insects that will eat it. Virginity and cheese consume themselves to the very rind, and so die with feeding their own stomach.

"Besides, virginity is peevish, proud, idle, and made of self-love, which is the most prohibited sin in the canon law. Don't keep your virginity; you cannot choose but lose by it, and so out with it! Within ten years a loss of virginity will make itself ten virgins, which is a goodly increase; and the principal itself — the former virgin — is not much the worse for the loss of her virginity, so away with virginity!"

Helena asked, "How might one do, sir, to lose it to her own liking?"

In other words, by what means could a woman lose her virginity to a man she loves in such a way that would be pleasing to her? What means could she use to do this? Her situation, of course, was that she would have to marry above her social station in order to lose her virginity to the man she loved. What means could be used to make that possible?

Parolles replied, "Let me see. How would she do? Indeed, she would do badly because she would like a man who never liked virginity."

According to Parolles, if a man takes away a woman's virginity, that man must dislike virginity.

He continued, "Virginity is a commodity that will lose the gloss with lying unused and untouched; the longer virginity is kept, the less virginity is worth. Off with it while it is sellable; answer the time of request and sell while there is a demand.

"Virginity, like an old courtier, wears her cap out of fashion. She is richly suited, but unsuitable, just like the brooch and the toothpick, which wear not now."

In other words, virginity is out of fashion, just like an old courtier who wears old fashions such as wearing a brooch or a toothpick in his cap. In this society, toothpicks were newfangled devices that came from Italy, and people used to wear them in their cap to show that they had traveled. At this time, this kind of showing off was out of fashion.

Parolles continued, "Your date is better in your pie and your porridge than in your cheek."

Dates are eighty percent sugar, and date sugar is simply ground-up dates. In this society, dates were often used instead of sugar to sweeten pies and porridge. Parolles' words, however, contained sexual innuendo. A date is phallic-shaped fruit, and "pie" is slang for "vagina." In addition, he was punning on the word "date," one meaning of which refers to age. It is better to have your date (fruit or penis) in your pie (food or vagina) than to have your date (age) appear in your cheeks in the form of wrinkles.

He continued, "And your virginity, your old virginity, is like one of our French withered pears. It looks ill, and it tastes dry; indeed, it is a withered pear; it was formerly better. Indeed, yet it is a withered pear."

He used the word "pear" to refer to the vulva.

Parolles then asked, "Will you do anything with your virginity?"

Helena replied, "I will not give up my virginity yet."

She thought, *I will not give up my virginity yet, yet there shall your master have a thousand loves.*

She was willing to give up her virginity to Bertram if she could marry him. Once she was married to him, he could enjoy her a thousand times. And since she was using the word "thousand" to refer to a large number rather than a specific number, she meant that he could enjoy her a thousand — and more — times.

She thought over what she would say next, and she decided to use the word "there" to mean two things: "in my vagina" and "in the court." In the court Bertram could meet many kinds of women with whom to have an affair. But if he were to marry Helena, she could play many loving roles for him. And if he were to enjoy her a thousand times, it would not be one experience repeated a thousand times but would instead be many kinds of loving experiences. She could fulfill the roles of the French lovers in the court.

Helena said out loud, "There shall your master have a thousand loves."

Helena wanted to keep her virginity until she was married, but at least some ladies in the French court would not be like her in that respect. Bertram would be tempted, and he could — and possibly would — fall.

She began to list the loves Bertram could enjoy: "A mother and a mistress and a friend, a phoenix, a Captain and an enemy, a guide, a goddess, and a sovereign, a counselor, a traitress, and a dear."

A phoenix is metaphorically a marvel; literally, the phoenix is a mythological bird, only one of which exists at a time. When the phoenix dies, it burns, and a new phoenix is born from the ashes.

Many of these terms came from the love poetry of the time and culture, as did these, including some oxymora she then mentioned: "His humble ambition, his proud humility. His jarring will be concord, and his discord will be dulcet. His faith will be sweet disaster."

A "disaster" is "an unlucky star or an unfavorable planet." This society believed in astrology and the belief that planets and stars can have a good or a bad effect on us.

Bertram could put his complete trust in a woman who would be a sweet disaster for him.

There were more names for the lovers whom Bertram could enjoy in the court of the French King. In addition to the names Helena had already mentioned, she now mentioned "a world of pretty, foolish, adopted Christian names, that blind Cupid, god of love, gives when he acts as a gossip — a godparent — and gives out names for infants at the baptismal font."

She hesitated and said, "Now shall he — I don't know what he shall. God send him good fortune! The court's a learning place, and he is one —"

Helena had not mentioned Bertram's name, so Parolles, confused, interrupted and asked, "Which one, in faith? Who are you talking about?"

"One whom I wish well," Helena said. "It is a pity …."

She stopped and sighed.

"What's a pity?" Parolles asked.

Helena replied, "It's a pity that wishing well does not have something tangible in it, which might be perceived, so that we, the poorer and lower born, whose baser and lower stars confine us to making wishes, might have real effects of our good wishes — that is, real and true and actually existing good fortune — follow our friends, and show what we can only think (rather than do), which never return us thanks."

In other words, she wished Bertram well, and she wished that her good wishes for him would come true. Unfortunately, wishing someone well often did not result in a wish come true, and simply wishing someone good fortune rather than being able to actually give someone good fortune was ungratifying.

A page entered the room and said, "Monsieur Parolles, my lord is calling for you. He wants to see you."

The page exited.

"Little Helen, farewell," Parolles said. "If I can remember you, I will think of you at court."

This was not very polite: *If* I can remember you!

Helena politely said, "Monsieur Parolles, you were born under a charitable star."

This society believed in astrology. On the surface, Helena was saying that Parolles was born under a star that governed kindness, and therefore Parolles shared in that characteristic and was kind. However, the charitable star could have been predominant or retrograde.

"I was born under Mars, I was," Parolles, who regarded himself as a military man, said.

"I especially think," Helena said, "that you were born under Mars."

"Why under Mars?" Parolles asked.

"The wars have so kept you under that you must necessarily have been born under Mars," Helena said.

"Kept you under" means "kept you in a lowly position." Parolles was a parasite, a hanger-on. He followed Bertram, who paid his expenses, around.

"When he was predominant," Parolles said.

"Predominant" means "in the ascendant" or "dominate."

"When he was retrograde, I think, rather."

"Retrograde" means "declining" or "moving in a contrary direction." A military man would prefer being born when the planet Mars is predominant. A person who wanted to be kind would prefer to be born when a charitable star is predominant.

"Why do you think so?"

"You go so much backward when you fight," Helena said.

In other words, he spent a lot of time retreating.

"That's for advantage," Parolles said.

In other words, those were tactical retreats.

In her reply, Helena used "advantage" as meaning "personal advantage."

"So is running away, when fear proposes one runs to reach safety; but the mixture that your valor and fear makes in you is a virtue of a good wing, and I like the wear — the fashion — well."

"A good wing" is "fast flight." Parolles retreated quickly.

Parolles replied, "I am so busy with business that I must attend to that I cannot answer you aptly. I will return from the court of the French King as a complete and perfect courtier.

"As a complete and perfect courtier, I will denaturize — educate — you so that you will be capable of hearing a courtier's counsel and understand what advice shall thrust upon you; otherwise, you will die in your unthankfulness, and your ignorance will do away with and destroy you."

Parolles' advice to Helena had been for her to give up her virginity. When he returned as a complete and perfect courtier, his advice would be the same. He would denaturize her; that is, he would change her nature so that she would no longer be a virgin. This kind of advice and denaturing would involve thrusting. Parolles equated virginity as being a kind of death, and his advice to her was to avoid that kind of death.

Parolles' words about being a complete and perfect courtier inspired him, and he gave good advice to Helena: "Farewell. When you have leisure, say your prayers; when you have no prayers left to say, remember your friends. Get yourself a good husband, and treat him as he treats you; since he is a good husband, he will treat you well. And so, I say farewell."

He exited.

Alone, Helena said to herself, "Our remedies often in ourselves lie, although we ascribe those remedies to Heaven. The fateful sky, aka Heaven, gives us free scope. It gives us free will, and it pulls backward our slow designs only when we ourselves are dull and sluggish.

"What power is it that raises my love so high — to one of Bertram's rank? What power is it that makes me see, and cannot feed my eye? In my mind I see what I want, but I am separated from it.

"The mightiest space in fortune, nature brings to join like likes and kiss like closely related things. Two people may be greatly different in personal fortune yet be so like likes — so compatible — that human nature will bring them together so that they can kiss."

In other words, human nature can bring together people who are vastly different in social class and yet are so compatible that they will kiss as if they were equals.

She continued, "Strange attempts are impossible to those who weigh their pains in sense and believe that what has been cannot be. People who sensibly count the costs of unusual courses of action think that such action is impossible, and they think that things that have actually happened cannot be real.

"Who has ever striven to show her merit who did fail to achieve her love?"

Helena believed in taking action. By taking meritable action, she believed that she could win her love.

She formulated a plan: "The King's disease — my plan may deceive me, but my goals are set and will not leave me. I have made up my mind, and I will put my plan into action."

In a room of the King of France's palace in Paris, the French King stood, holding a letter. With him were many lords and attendants. At this time, the people of Florence and Siena, two cities in the Tuscan region of Italy, were at war against each other.

The King said, "The Florentines and Sienese are by the ears; they have fought with equal fortune and continue a defiant war that is full of boasting on both sides."

"By the ears" meant "fighting like beasts"; some animals when fighting will go for their opponents' ears.

"So it is reported, sir," the first lord said.

"The report is most credible and believable," the King said.

Using the royal plural, he said, "We here consider it a certainty; our cousin the King of Austria vouches for it."

In this culture, a monarch often used the word "cousin" to refer to another monarch. The word did not mean that they were related; it simply meant that they were fellow monarchs.

The King continued, "The King of Austria cautions us that the Florentines will appeal to us for speedy aid. Concerning this, our dearest friend prejudges the business and would seem to have us deny this request."

The first lord said to the King of Austria, "His love and wisdom, of which your majesty has proof, may plead for amplest credence. His love and wisdom are evidence that you should carefully consider what he writes."

"He has armed our answer," the French King said, "and the Duke of Florence is denied before he comes here. Yet, for our gentlemen who mean to fight in the Tuscan war, they freely have our royal permission to fight on either side."

"This war may well serve as a training ground for our gentry, who are longing for military exercise and exploit."

The King looked up and asked, "Who is he who is coming here?"

Bertram, Lafeu, and Parolles entered the room.

"It is the Count Rousillon, my good lord," the first lord said. "It is young Bertram."

The King said to Bertram, "Youth, you have your father's face. Generous nature, rather with carefulness than in haste, has well composed and produced you. May you inherit your father's moral character, too! Welcome to Paris."

"My thanks and duty are your majesty's," Bertram said.

"I wish I had that bodily soundness — health — now that I had when your father and myself in friendship first tried our soldiership! Your father had a deep knowledge of the military service of the time and the bravest and most excellent soldiers were his disciples.

"He lasted long, but haggish age stole on us both and wore us out so that we were out of action.

"It much restores me to talk about your good father. In his youth he had the wit that I can well observe today in our young lords, but they may jest until their own scorn returns to them unnoted before they can hide their levity in honor. Young lords today laugh so much at other people that they don't realize that other people laugh at them; fortunately, they grow up and become honorable and stop laughing at other people. Your father never laughed at others.

"Your father was like a courtier. His pride was not touched with contempt toward other people, and his sharpness of intellect was not touched with bitterness toward other people. If they ever were touched with these qualities, it was your father's social equal who brought them into being, and your father's honor, acting as a clock to itself, knew the true minute — the right time — when his sense of grievance bid him to speak up, and at this time his tongue obeyed his hand. His tongue said only what the hand of his clock of honor bid him to say — he did not overstate or understate his grievance but said only the right thing.

"Those who were below him in social rank he treated as creatures of another place — he treated them as if they were of a higher social rank than they actually had. And he bowed his eminent head to their low ranks, making them proud of his humility. He was humble as he received the praise of the poor.

"Such a man might be an example to these younger times; if his example were followed well, it would demonstrate to these young lords that they now are regressing and becoming worse."

Bertram replied, "The memory of my good father, sir, lies richer in your thoughts than on his tomb. The attestation and affirmation of my father's good character lives not in his epitaph as much as it does in your royal speech."

"I wish I were with him!" the King said. "He would always say ... I think I hear him say it now; his praiseworthy words he scattered not superficially in ears, but grafted and implanted his words to make them grow there and to bear fruit ... 'Let me not live' ... this his good melancholy often began at the end and conclusion of an entertainment, when it was over and out. 'Let me not live,' said he, 'after my flame lacks oil, to be the snuff — the charred wick hindering further burning — of younger spirits, whose apprehensive and perceptive senses disdain all but new things; whose minds are completely occupied with devising new fashions of clothing and whose loyalties expire before their fashions.'

"This he wished. I after him do after him wish the same thing, too — I survived him, but I follow him in wishing for the same thing. Since I can bring home neither wax nor honey, I wish that I quickly were set free from my hive, to give some laborers room."

"You are loved, sir," the second lord said. "They who least lend love to you shall lack you first. Those who least love you will miss you first."

"I fill a place, I know it," the French King replied. He wanted to die, to vacate the place he filled.

He then asked Bertram, the Count of Rousillon, "How long has it been, Count, since the physician at your father's palace died? He was very famous."

"He died some six months ago, my lord."

"If he were still living, I would try him and see if he could cure my illness," the King said. "Lend me an arm; the other doctors have worn me out with several different medical treatments; nature and sickness contend over my illness at their leisure.

"Welcome, Count. My son's no dearer to me than you are."

"I thank your majesty," Bertram replied.

The Countess, a Steward, and a professional Fool, whose job was to entertain the Countess, were in a room of the palace in Rousillon.

The Countess said to the Steward, "I will now hear what you have to say about this gentlewoman: Helena."

The Steward replied, "Madam, the care I have had to make your life even and unruffled I wish might be found in the record of my past endeavors because we wound our modesty and make foul the clearness of our deservings, when of ourselves we ourselves publish them. People ought not to praise their own good deeds and qualities."

By mentioning "publish," aka "making known publicly," the Steward was hinting that what he had to say ought to be said in private. He did not want the Fool present when he talked about Helena.

Getting the hint, the Countess looked around and noticed the Fool. She said, "What is this knave doing here? Get you gone, sirrah."

"Sirrah" was a way of addressing a male of lower social rank than the speaker.

Although the Fool had a lower social rank than the Countess, the Fool did have privileges, such as being able to speak frankly to those of a higher social rank. This Fool took advantage of that privilege and did not leave immediately. He would use the opportunity to engage in foolery, and then he would leave.

The Countess continued, "The complaints I have heard of you I do not all believe, but it is because of my slowness and lack of mental acuity that I do not because I know that you don't lack the folly to commit them and I know that you have ability enough to make such knaveries yours. You are both a fool and a knave."

"It is not unknown to you, madam, that I am a poor fellow," the Fool said.

"Well, and so what of it, sir?" the Countess asked.

"No, madam, it is not so well that I am poor, although many of the rich are damned, but if I may have your ladyship's good will to go to the world, Isbel the serving woman and I will do as we may."

"To go to the world" meant "to get married." The Fool wanted to do as married people in the world do: "To do" meant "to have sex."

"Will you need to be a beggar?" the Countess asked, aware that having a wife involves expenses.

"I beg your good will in this case," the Fool answered.

"In what case?" the Countess asked.

"In Isbel's case and my own," the Fool said.

In this society, one meaning of the word "case" was "vagina."

The Fool continued, "Service is no heritage."

This proverb meant that servants neither inherit an estate nor leave behind an estate to be inherited after they die.

The Fool continued, "And I think I shall never have the blessing of God until I have issue of my body; that is, until I have children. People say that bairns — children — are blessings."

"Tell me your reason why you will marry," the Countess said.

"My poor body, madam, requires it," the Fool replied. "I am driven on by the flesh; and he must needs go whom the Devil drives."

"Is this all your worship's reason?" the Countess asked.

"Indeed, madam, I have other holy reasons such as they are," the Fool said.

The Fool was punning. "Holy" referred to "hole," or "vagina." In this culture, the word "reasons" was pronounced much like the word "raisings," which in this context referred to "erections."

"May the world know those holy reasons?" the Countess asked.

"I have been, madam, a wicked creature, as you and all flesh and blood are," the Fool replied, "and, indeed, I marry so that I may repent."

"You will repent your marriage sooner than you repent your wickedness," the Countess said.

"I am out of friends, madam, and I hope to have friends for my wife's sake," the Fool said.

"Such friends are your enemies, knave," the Countess said.

Such friends would commit adultery with his wife.

"You're shallow and superficial, madam, in judging great friends," the Fool said, "for the knaves come to do that for me which I am weary of. He who plows my land spares my team and gives me leave to bring in the crop; if I be his cuckold, he's my drudge."

The Fool was speaking metaphorically. Other men would plow his wife and allow him to bring in the harvest: a child. By doing his plowing for him, the other men would make the Fool a cuckold: a man with an unfaithful wife.

He was also willing to completely reverse his position in order to create comedy. Just a moment ago, he had said that he desperately wanted to marry Isbel so he could have sex with her. Now he was talking about being weary of having sex with Isbel and therefore being happy when other men did his husbandly duty.

The Fool said, "He who comforts my wife is the cherisher of my flesh and blood; he who cherishes my flesh and blood loves my flesh and blood; he who loves my flesh and blood is my friend; ergo, he who kisses my wife is my friend. If married men could be contented to be what they are — cuckolds — there would be no fear in marriage.

"Young Charbon the Puritan and old Poysam the Catholic Papist, however much their hearts are severed in religion, their heads are both one and the same — horned. They may knock horns together, like any deer in the herd."

"Charbon" means "good meat," and "poysam" means fish. In this culture, Puritans ate meat and Catholics ate fish on Fridays. But married Puritan men and married Catholic men, despite their difference in religion, are alike in being cuckolds — according to the Fool, all married men are cuckolds. Cuckolds were said to have horns that were invisible to them.

The Countess asked the Fool, "Will you always be a foul-mouthed and calumnious knave?"

"I am a prophet, madam; and I speak the truth the nearest, shortest, most direct way," the Fool said.

He sang:

"*For I the ballad will repeat,*

"*Which men very true shall find:*

"*Your marriage comes by destiny,*

"*Your cuckoo sings by kind.*"

A man marries by individual destiny, but when it comes to a cuckoo singing its song to a married man, that is something that happens by nature — it is natural for every married man to become a cuckold and therefore it is natural for the cuckoo to sing its song to mock him.

Cuckoo birds were thought to mock cuckolds by singing, "Cuckoo! Cuckoo!" Cuckoos lay their eggs in other birds' nests, and so the other birds end up raising the cuckoos' offspring.

"Get you gone, sir," the Countess said to the Fool. "I'll talk more with you soon."

"May it please you, madam, that he tells Helen to come to you," the Steward said. "I am going to speak to you about her."

The Countess said to the Fool, "Sirrah, tell my gentlewoman that I want to speak with her. Helen, I mean."

The Fool sang:

"Was this fair face the cause, quoth [said] she,

"Why the Grecians sacked Troy?

"Fond [Foolishly] done, done fond [foolishly],

"Was this King Priam's joy?

"With that she sighed as she stood,

"With that she sighed as she stood,

"And gave this sentence [wise saying] then;

"Among nine bad if one be good,

"Among nine bad if one be good,

"There's yet one good in ten."

In Christopher Marlowe's play *Doctor Faustus*, Faust says these lines to a demonic spirit impersonating Helen of Troy:

"Was this the face that launch'd a thousand ships,

"And burnt the topless towers of Ilium?

"Sweet Helen, make me immortal with a kiss.

"Her lips suck forth my soul: see, where it flies!

"Come, Helen, come, give me my soul again.

"Here will I dwell, for Heaven is in these lips,

"And all is dross that is not Helena.

"I will be Paris, and for love of thee,

"Instead of Troy, shall Wittenberg be sack'd;

"And I will combat with weak Menelaus,

"And wear thy colours on my plumed crest;

"Yea, I will wound Achilles in the heel,

"And then return to Helen for a kiss.

"O, thou art fairer than the evening air

"Clad in the beauty of a thousand stars;

"Brighter art thou than flaming Jupiter

"When he appear'd to hapless Semele;

"More lovely than the monarch of the sky

"In wanton Arethusa's azur'd arms;

"And none but thou shalt be my paramour!"

The Fool's song and Marlowe's poetry were in part about the Trojan War. Paris, Prince of Troy, had foolishly run away with Helen, the wife of King Menelaus of Sparta, and brought her back to Troy. The Trojan War was fought to get Helen of Troy back for her legal husband.

"Ilium" is another name for "Troy."

In the Trojan War, Achilles, the greatest Greek warrior, died after a poisoned arrow struck his heel.

Semele was the mortal mother of the god Bacchus; Jupiter, King of the gods, was his father. He promised to give Semele anything she wanted if she would sleep with him. After they had slept together, she told him that she wanted to see him in his full divine glory rather than just in the form he took when he appeared to mortals. Because he had sworn an inviolable oath, he did as she requested. Unable to endure the sight, she burst into flames. She was already pregnant with Bacchus, but Jupiter rescued the fetus and sewed it in his thigh until it was ready to be born. Because Bacchus had been "born" from an immortal god, Bacchus was himself an immortal god.

Arethusa was a nymph who was pursued by the river-god Alpheus. In Ovid's *Metamorphoses*, she was transformed into a stream. According to Marlowe's poem, she had sex with Jupiter, god of the sky.

"One good in ten?" the Countess said. "You corrupt the song, sirrah."

She knew that the Fool's song really ended in this way:

"Among nine good if one be bad,

"There's yet nine good in ten."

The original song had presumably been about men — King Priam's sons born to his Queen, Hecuba — but the Fool clarified that he was singing about women.

The Fool replied, "One good woman in ten, madam; this is a purifying of the song. I wish that God would serve the world so all the year! We would find no fault with the tithe-woman, if I were the parson."

The parson was entitled to take possession of the tithe-pig: one pig in every ten. The Fool was saying that if he were the parson he would be happy if one woman out of ten was a good woman.

The Fool continued, "One in ten, did he say! If we might have a good woman born every time a blazing star — a comet or a nova — was seen or every time an earthquake occurred, it would mend the lottery well — it would improve the odds of a man finding a good woman to be his wife. Right now, a man may draw his heart out before he plucks a good woman out of the lottery that is marriage."

"You'll be gone, Sir Knave, and do as I command you," the Countess said.

"That man should be at woman's command, and yet no hurt done!" the Fool said.

In 1 Corinthians 11:13, St. Paul wrote this: "But I would have you know, that the head of every man is Christ; and the head of the woman is the man; and the head of Christ is God" (King James Version).

The Fool continued, "Though honesty be no Puritan, yet it will do no hurt; it will wear the surplice of humility over the black gown of a proud heart."

In this society, laws required ministers to wear a surplice, a white linen vestment worn by Anglicans. Puritan ministers often wore a Genevan black gown, the clerical garb of Calvinists, under the white surplice. Thus, they rebelled under a show of obeying the law.

The Fool was saying that he would obey the Countess' orders, but that he would continue to do his job as a Fool: to make her laugh and to provide satire — humorous criticism — as necessary.

The Fool said, "I am going, indeed. The business is for Helen to come hither. I will go and get her."

He exited.

"Well, now," the Countess said.

"I know, madam," the Steward said. "I know that you love your gentlewoman Helen entirely and sincerely."

"Indeed, I do," the Countess said. "Her father bequeathed her to me, and she herself, without other advantage, may lawfully make title to as much love as she finds. More is owing to her than has been paid to her, and more shall be paid to her than she'll demand."

The Countess was using financial language. "Bequeathed" means "bestowed [like property]." "Advantage" means "financial profit or interest." "Title" means "legal possession."

Definitely, the Countess thought very highly of Helena.

The Steward said, "Madam, I was very recently much closer to her than I think she wished me. She was alone, and she was talking to herself. She thought, I dare say, that she did not know that her words were reaching any other person's ears.

"The content of her talk was that she loved your son, Bertram. Lady Fortune, she said, was no goddess, not when she had put such difference between her estate and Bertram's estate.

"Love, she said, was no god, not when he would not exert his might except only where social ranks were even.

"Diana, she said, was no Queen of virgins, not when she would allow her poor knight — Helena herself — to be surprised and captured, without Diana providing a rescue in the first assault or a ransom afterward.

"These words Helena delivered in the most bitter depth of pain and sorrow that I ever heard a virgin exclaim. This I held my duty to speedily acquaint you with, since, in the loss — the loss of Helena's virginity, or the loss of your son in marriage — that may happen, it concerns you to know it."

"You have performed this honestly," the Countess said. "Keep it to yourself. Many signs informed me of this previously, but they hung so tottering in the balance that I could neither believe nor misdoubt. I was unable to be sure that Helena loved my son or that Helena did not love my son. Please, leave me. Keep this information in your bosom and don't share it. I thank you for your honest care, and I will soon speak further with you."

The Steward exited.

Helena entered the room.

The Countess said quietly to herself, "Even so it was with me when I was young. I was in love then just like Helena is now. If ever we are nature's, these pangs of love are ours. This thorn rightly belongs to our rose of youth — it is natural to fall in love, although falling in love brings pain. We are born with red blood, and passionate disposition is born in that blood. A passionate disposition is the show and seal of nature's truth, where love's strong passion is imprinted in youth. It is entirely natural to be passionate when one is young. We remember days long past, and we know that our passions were our faults, but we did not think then that they were faults.

"Helena's eye is sick with love. I see that she is now in love."

"What is your pleasure, madam?" Helena asked. "What do you want?"

"You know, Helen, that I am a mother to you," the Countess replied.

"You are my honorable mistress," Helena said.

Among other definitions, a mistress is a woman who is the guardian of a minor.

Helena did not want to call the Countess her mother because if the Countess were her mother, then Bertram would be her brother and she could never marry him. She would, however, like for the Countess to be her mother-in-law.

"No, I am a mother," the Countess said. "Why not a mother? When I said 'a mother,' I thought you reacted as if you saw a serpent. What's in the word 'mother' that you startle when you hear it? I say that I am your mother, and I put you in the catalogue of those who were born from my womb.

"It is often seen that adoption strives with nature and choice breeds a native slip to us from foreign seeds. Through adoption we make our own what was previously foreign."

She was comparing adopting a child to grafting a branch onto a tree.

The Countess continued, "You never oppressed and troubled me with a mother's groan in childbirth, yet I express to you a mother's care. God's mercy, maiden! Does it curdle your blood to say I am your mother?"

Helena began to cry.

The Countess said, "What's the matter that causes this distempered messenger of wet, the many-colored Iris, goddess of the rainbow, which is created by light shining through drops of water, to round your eye? Why shed tears? Why? Because you are my daughter?"

"Because I am not," Helena said.

She meant that she was crying because she was not the Countess' daughter-in-law.

The Countess said, "I say, I am your mother."

"Pardon me, madam," Helena replied. "The Count Rousillon cannot be my brother. I have a humble origin; his family has an honored name. My parents have no great social standing; his are all noble. My master is my dear lord, and I live as his servant, and I will die as his vassal. He must not be my brother."

"Then I must not be your mother?" the Countess asked.

"You are my mother, madam," Helena said. "I wish you were — as long as my lord your son were not my brother — indeed my mother!"

She wanted the Countess to be her mother-in-law, but she was unwilling to openly say this.

Helena continued, "Or if you were the mother of us both, I would care no more for it than I do for Heaven, as long as I were not his sister."

Perhaps Helena meant that it is impossible to love something more than Heaven and that she would love having the Countess as her mother-in-law equally as much as she loved Heaven.

Helena still was not willing to speak openly of her love for Bertram. If she had been willing, she might have said, "Or if you were the mother of us both, I would care no *less* for it than I do for Heaven, as long as I were not his sister." Or perhaps she might not have said that. Soon, Helena would say that she loved Heaven first, Bertram second, and the Countess third.

Helena cared for Heaven; if the Countess were Helena's mother-in-law and Bertram's mother, it would be Heavenly.

She continued, "Is there no other option? Must I, being your daughter, have him as my brother?"

"Yes, Helen, there is another option: You might be my daughter-in-law," the Countess said. "God forbid that you don't mean it! God forbid that you don't mean that you love my son!"

The Countess wanted to have Helena as her daughter-in-law.

She continued, "The words 'daughter' and 'mother' make your pulse race. What, pale in your face again? My fear has caught your fondness."

The Countess' fear was that Helena might not love her son. Helena reacted with paleness to the Countess' acknowledgement that she knew that Helena loved her son.

The Countess continued, "Now I see the mystery of your loneliness, and I find the source of your salt tears. Now to all my senses it is completely obvious that you love my son. Fabricated excuses are ashamed, against the proclamation of your passion, to say you do not love my son. I am completely unable to say that.

"Therefore tell me the truth, but tell me then that it is so, that you do love my son. For, look, your cheeks confess, the one to the other that you love my son, and your eyes see your love for my son so obviously shown in your behaviors that in your eyes' own manner — by weeping — they speak it.

"Only sin and hellish obstinacy tie your tongue, making it so that truth should be doubted.

"Speak, is it so? Do you love my son? If it is so, you have wound a fine ball of yarn."

Winding a fine ball of yarn is a positive image. Once the yarn is wound into a ball, it won't get tangled. Having a son soon married to a good woman is a good thing.

The Countess continued, "If it is not so, forswear and deny it; however, I charge you as Heaven shall work in me on your behalf, tell me truly."

"Good madam, pardon me!" Helena cried.

"Do you love my son?" the Countess asked.

"Give me your pardon, noble mistress!" Helena pleaded.

"Do you love my son?" the Countess asked again.

"Don't you love him, madam?" Helena asked.

"Don't try to avoid answering the question," the Countess said. "My love has in it a bond of which the world takes note. My love for him is that of a mother for her son. Come, come, disclose to me the state of your affection, for your passions have to the full informed against you."

Helena knelt and said, "Then, I confess, here on my knee, before high Heaven and you, that more than I love you, and next to the love I have for high Heaven, I love your son.

"My relatives were poor, but honest; so is my love. Don't be offended, for it doesn't hurt him to be loved by me. I don't follow him with any token of presumptuous wooing, nor would I have him until I deserve him, yet I shall never know how that desert should be earned.

"I know I love in vain and strive against hope, yet in this captious and inteemable sieve that is hope I still pour in the waters of my love and lack not to lose still."

The word "captious" means both "capacious" and "deceptive." The word "inteemable" means "unretentive."

She was saying that her hope of marrying Bertram is a sieve that "takes in" in two senses: 1) it takes in all the emotion and love she pours into it (the sieve is capacious), and 2) it takes her in — it fools her into thinking, aka hoping, that marrying Bertram is possible (the sieve is deceptive). Because it is a sieve, it is unretentive — it does not retain water (or love) and it can never be filled up.

Helena continued, "Thus, Indian-like, religious in my error, I adore the Sun, which looks upon his worshipper but knows of him no more."

She meant that she looked at and loved Bertram, but although Bertram sometimes saw her, he knew little about her — he certainly did not know that she loved him.

Helena continued, "My dearest madam, let not your hate encounter with my love for loving where you do, but if you yourself, whose aged honor is evidence of a virtuous youth, did ever in so true a flame of liking wish chastely and love dearly that your Diana was both herself and love — that Diana was the goddess both of chastity and of love — oh, then, give pity to a woman — me — whose state is such that she cannot choose but lend and give love where she is sure to lose, a woman — me — who seeks not to find that which her search implies, but riddle-like lives sweetly where she dies! I seek only to love your son and live where he lives so I can at least see him and be happy in that although I know that I cannot marry him and that makes me feel like dying."

The Countess was intelligent. Bertram was in Paris, and Helena wanted to be where Bertram was, and so the Countess asked, "Haven't you had recently the intention — tell me the truth — of going to Paris?"

"Yes, madam, I have."

"Why? Tell me the truth."

"I will tell you the truth," Helena said. "By grace itself I swear I will. You know that my father left me some prescriptions — instructions on how to make medicines — of rare and proven effects, such as his reading and true experience had collected for general effectiveness, and you know that he desired me to carefully preserve them and employ and distribute them, as these are prescriptions whose great powers are greater than are generally recognized. Among all these prescriptions, there is a remedy, proven and set down, to cure the desperate languishings that the King suffers from and which are thought will kill him."

"This was your motive to go to Paris, was it?" the Countess asked. Helena had not mentioned her son. She commanded, "Speak."

Helena said, "My lord your son made me think of this; otherwise, Paris and the medicine and the King would perhaps have been absent from the conversation of my thoughts."

"Do you think, Helen," the Countess said, "that if you should offer your supposed aid, the King would receive it? He and his physicians are of the same mind. He believes that his physicians cannot help him, and they believe that they cannot help him. How then shall they give any credence to a poor unlearned virgin, when the schools, which have emptied their learning into the physicians, have left the King's disease to run its own course?"

"Here's something more than my father's skill, which was the greatest of his profession," Helena said, "and that is that his good prescription shall because of my legacy be sanctified by the luckiest stars in Heaven."

Her legacy was that she was the daughter of the greatest physician of her father's time. Because of her father's skill, and because she was the daughter of her father, it made sense to think that the Heavens would smile on her attempt to cure the King.

Helena continued, "If your honor would only give me permission to try my success at curing the King, I would venture the well-lost — lost in a good cause, if I should lose — life of mine on his grace's cure by such a day and hour."

"Do you believe you can cure the King?" the Countess asked.

"Yes, madam; in fact, I know I can."

"Why, Helen, you shall have my permission and love, means and attendants, and my loving greetings to those of my family and friends in court. I'll stay at home and pray for God's blessing on your attempt to cure the King. Leave tomorrow, and be sure of this, whatever I can do to help you, you shall not miss."

CHAPTER 2

— 2.1 —

The King of France and many young lords who were leaving to go to Italy and fight on the side of the Florentines or on the side of the Sienese were in a room in the King's palace. Bertram and Parolles were also present.

The King of France said, "Farewell, young lords. Do not throw away from you these warlike principles I have told you. And you, the other group of my young lords, farewell. Share my advice between you; if both groups of young lords gain by my advice, then my gift stretches itself as it is received, and the gift is enough for both groups."

The first lord said, "It is our hope, sir, after we have well entered the lists of soldiers, to return to Paris and find your grace in health."

"No, no, that cannot be," the King said, "and yet my heart will not confess that it has the malady that is besieging my life.

"Farewell, young lords; whether I live or die, may you be the sons of worthy Frenchmen. Let the upper class of Italy, excepting some men, see that you come not to woo honor, but to wed it. Those men I except are those who inherit only the fall from a high place of the last monarchy, that of the Holy Roman Empire; such men are bated, aka lowered or lessened in position, because they do not live up to the ideals of their ancestors. They inherit only the physical part of their ancestors but not their morals or virtues. When the bravest quester shrinks, find what you seek, so that the goddess Fame may cry your name out loud. I say, farewell."

The second lord said, "May health serve your majesty and do your bidding!"

The King said, "Those girls of Italy, take heed of them: They say that our Frenchmen lack language to deny them, if they make demands. Beware of becoming captives to love, before you serve in war."

Both groups of lords said, "Our hearts receive your warnings."

"Farewell," the King said.

He then said to some lords, "Come over here to me."

The King and some of the lords talked together quietly.

Bertram, Parolles, and two lords also talked together.

The first lord said to Bertram, "Oh, my sweet lord, it's a pity that you will stay behind and not go with us to the war!"

Parolles interrupted, "It is not his fault, the spark."

A "spark" is a "young dude" or "young man about town."

The second lord said, "Oh, it will be a brave and splendid war!"

"It will be very admirable," Parolles said. "I have seen those wars."

Bertram said, "The King has commanded me to stay here, and he has made a fuss about me being 'too young' and telling me 'next year' and 'it is too early for you to go to war.'"

Parolles said, "If your mind is resolved to go to the war, boy, steal away bravely and go to the war in Tuscany anyway."

Bertram replied, "I shall stay here and be the foremost horse in a team of horses led by a woman. I will squeak my shoes as I dance on the flat masonry, until all honor has been entirely purchased by the soldiers in Italy, and I will wear no sword except the decorative sword that gentlemen wear at dances! By Heaven, I'll steal away."

"There's honor in that kind of theft," the first lord said.

"Commit the theft, Count," Parolles said.

Bertram was the Count of Rousillon.

"I am your accessary and assistant; and so, farewell," the second lord said.

Bertram replied, "I am growing deeply attached to you, and our parting is like a body being torn in half."

"Farewell, Captain," the first lord said.

Bertram was the Captain.

"Sweet Monsieur Parolles!" the second lord said.

Parolles replied, "Noble heroes, my sword and yours are kin. Good and lustrous sparks, a word. You are good metals with good mettle.

"You shall find in the regiment of the Spinii one Captain Spurio, with his scar, an emblem of war, here on his sinister — left — cheek; it was this very sword I am holding that entrenched it on that cheek. Say to him that I live, and observe his reaction for me."

"We shall, noble Captain," the first lord said.

The lords exited.

"May Mars be fond of you as his apprentices!" Parolles said to the departing lords.

He then asked Bertram about his plans: "What will you do?"

An excited Bertram had thought about stealing away and going to the Tuscan war, but a calmer Bertram said now, "I will stay here and serve the King."

Parolles said, "Show a more ample courtesy to the noble lords; you have restrained yourself within the bounds of too cold an adieu. Be more expressive to and unrestrained with them, for they are the ornaments on the cap of the times. They are walking on the right — the popular and fashionable — path, and they eat, speak, and move under the influence of the most popular and fashionable star. Even if the Devil should lead the dance, such leaders are to be followed. Go after them, and make a more prolonged farewell."

"I will be sure to do so," Bertram replied.

"They are worthy fellows," Parolles said, "and they are likely to prove to be most muscular swordsmen."

Bertram and Parolles exited.

Lafeu entered the room, knelt, and said, "I ask pardon, my lord, for myself and for my tidings."

"I'll fee you to stand up," the King replied.

This meant that the King would reward him to stand up.

"Then here's a man who is standing, who has bought his pardon," Lafeu replied.

He was like a man who had taken money from the King and bought his pardon.

Lafeu added, "I wish you had kneeled, my lord, to ask me mercy, and that at my bidding you could stand up."

The King, who was so ill that he could not kneel and then stand up again without assistance, replied, "I wish I had so that I could have broken your head, and asked your mercy for breaking it."

"Indeed, across," Lafeu said.

They were friendly enough that they could joust verbally. By saying "across," Lafeu was saying that the King had not jousted well — his joking was not all that funny. When a jouster's lance hits his opponent across, it is not well aimed and is not straight.

Lafeu continued, "But, my good lord, this is what I came here for: Do you want to be cured of your infirmity?"

"No," the King said bluntly. He had given up hope that he could be cured.

"Will you eat no grapes, my royal fox?" Lafeu said.

He was referring to one of Aesop's fables: A fox wanted to eat grapes that were hanging from a vine, but he could not reach them, and so he said, "I bet those grapes were sour, anyway."

Lafeu added, "Yes, but you will eat my noble grapes, if my royal fox could reach them. I have good news: The grapes are within your reach. I have seen a medicine that's able to breathe life into a stone, make a rock come alive, and make you dance a lively canary dance with spritely fire and motion. This medicine's simple touch is powerful enough to raise King Pepin from the dead, and to give his son, great Charlemagne, a pen in his hand, and write to her a love letter."

"What 'her' is this?" the King asked.

"Why, Doctor She," Lafeu replied. "My lord, there's a woman arrived, if you will see her. Now, by my faith and honor, if I may seriously convey my thoughts in this my light speech, I have spoken with one who in her sex, years, profession of what she is able to accomplish, wisdom, and constancy has amazed me more than I dare blame my weakness due to old age. The amazement I feel because of her I cannot lay to my old age. Will you see her? That is her request. Will you know her business?"

The King was smiling because Lafeu's praise of Doctor She was so enthusiastic.

Lafeu said, "Once you have done that, then feel free to laugh well at me."

"Now, good Lafeu, bring in the Doctor She who has so filled you with admiration. We with you will utter our wonder, too, or take away your wonder by wondering how you came to have it."

"I'll satisfy you that my wonder is deserved, and I won't be all day about it either."

He went to the door, just outside of which Helena — Doctor She — was waiting.

The King said, "Thus he always introduces his special trifles."

Lafeu returned with Helena, who was shy and apprehensive in the presence of the King.

Lafeu said to Helena, "Come along."

"This haste has wings indeed," the King said sarcastically.

"Come along," Lafeu repeated. "This is his majesty; say what you have to say to him. You are so apprehensive that you look like a traitor, but such traitors his majesty seldom fears. I am Cressida's uncle, and I dare to leave you two alone together; fare you well."

Cressida's uncle was Pandarus. During the Trojan War, he was the go-between for Cressida and her lover, Troilus. From Pandarus' name we get the words "pander" and "pandar."

Lafeu exited.

Using the royal plural, the King said, "Now, fair one, does your business pertain to us?"

"Yes, my good lord," Helena replied. "Gerard de Narbon was my father; he had an established reputation as a physician."

"I knew him," the King said.

"Then I will omit my praises about my father," Helena said. "You knew him, and so you know his good qualities. When he was on his deathbed, he gave me many written instructions for making various medicines. One medicine in particular was the dearest outcome of his medical practice, and of his old experience the only darling. This medicine he bade me store up, as if it were a third eye — as if it were as valuable as eyesight that brought special knowledge. He wanted me to keep this medicine safer than my own two eyes; he regarded this medicine as dearer than my own two eyes.

"I did as my father asked, and hearing that your high majesty is infected with that malignant disease which the honor of my dear father's gift stands chief in power to cure, I come to offer this medicine and my medical care with all dutiful humbleness."

"We thank you, maiden," the King said, using the royal plural. "But we may not be so believing in a cure, when our most learned doctors leave us, saying that they cannot help us, and when the physicians of the congregated college have concluded that the laboring medical art can never ransom life when the ill body that contains it is not aidable.

"I say we must not so stain our judgment, or hope foolishly, to prostitute our past-cure malady to medical quacks, or to divorce our great self and our reputation by behaving in an unroyal fashion and esteeming and valuing a senseless help when such help we deem to be past sense and irrational."

"My duty then shall pay me for my pains," Helena said. "I will no longer try to force my services on you, but I humbly entreat from your royal thoughts a modest one that I can bear with me when I go back home again."

As a young, single woman, Helena was modest. She was worried about appearing to be immodest by appearing before and talking to the King, and she wanted an acknowledgement from him that she had acted with good motives.

"I cannot give you less," the King said. "I am grateful. You thought to help me; and such thanks I give as one near death gives to those who wish him to live. But what I know fully, you know no part; I know all my peril, and you know no medical art."

Helena replied, "What I can do can do you no harm to try, since you fully believe there is no cure and that you will die.

"He who of greatest works is finisher often does them by the weakest minister. So Holy Scripture in babes has judgment shown, when judges have been babes; great floods have flowed from simple sources, and great seas have dried when miracles have by the greatest been denied."

1 Corinthians 1:27 states, "But God hath chosen the foolish things of the world to confound the wise; and God hath chosen the weak things of the world to confound the things which are mighty" (King James Version).

Psalm 8:2 states, "Out of the mouth of babes and sucklings hast thou ordained strength because of thine enemies, that thou mightest still the enemy and the avenger" (King James Version).

Matthew 11:25 states, "At that time Jesus answered and said, I thank thee, O Father, Lord of heaven and earth, because thou hast hid these things from the wise and prudent, and hast revealed them unto babes" (King James Version).

Exodus 17:6 states, "Behold, I will stand before thee there upon the rock in Horeb; and thou shalt smite the rock, and there shall come water out of it, that the people may drink. And Moses did so in the sight of the elders of Israel" (King James Version).

Exodus 14:16, 21-22 states, "But lift thou up thy rod, and stretch out thine hand over the sea, and divide it: and the children of Israel shall go on dry ground through the midst of the sea. [...] And Moses stretched out his hand over the sea; and the Lord caused the sea to go back by a strong east wind all that night, and made the sea dry land, and the waters were divided. / And the children of Israel went into the midst of the sea upon the dry ground: and the waters were a wall unto them on their right hand, and on their left" (King James Bible).

In Exodus, the great Pharaoh of Egypt was unable to perform miracles, but God gave Moses the power to perform miracles.

Helena continued, "Often expectation fails and most often it fails there where most it promises, and often it hits where hope is coldest and despair most fits. Sometimes we get what we want after we have given up hope of getting it."

The King replied, "I must not listen to you. Fare you well, kind maiden. You must pay yourself when your pains are not accepted and used. Offers not taken reap only thanks for their reward."

Helena said, "Divinely inspired good deeds thus by speech are barred. It is not so with Him Who knows all things as it is with us who shape our guesses about reality by superficial appearances. But we are most presumptuous when we mistake the help of Heaven for the act of men."

Helena was implicitly comparing herself to an Old Testament prophet who was being turned away from a King.

She continued, "Dear sir, to my endeavors give consent. Of Heaven, not me, make an experiment. I am not an impostor who proclaims that I will do something that I cannot do. You should know that I think and you should think that I know most certainly that my medical knowledge is not lacking in power nor are you past cure. I am confident that my medicine will cure you."

"Are you so confident?" the King asked. "Within what space of time do you hope I will be cured?"

Helena replied, "With the greatest Grace — God — lending grace, aka mercy, you shall be cured before twice the horses of the sun shall bring their fiery torchbearer his daily ring. You shall be cured before twice in murk and western damp moist Hesperus — Venus, the evening star — has quenched her sleepy lamp by sinking into the western sea. Or you shall be cured before four and twenty times the pilot's hourglass has told how the thievish minutes pass. Within one day, or two days, what is infirm shall fly away from your sound parts, health shall live free and sickness shall freely — readily — die."

"What do you dare venture upon your certainty and confidence that I will be cured?" the King asked.

Helena replied, "If I fail to cure you, then accuse me of impudence, of having the boldness of a strumpet. Let my shame be publicly proclaimed. Let my maiden's name be calumniated by odious ballads sung about me. In addition, let my reputation be seared and branded in other ways. And, worse, if it is in fact worse than losing my maidenly reputation, let my life be ended with vilest torture by prolonged and extended stretching of my body on the rack."

The King said, "I think that some blessed spirit speaks his powerful sound within you, who are a weak organ. And what impossibility would slay in common sense, sense saves another way — what common sense says is impossible, a different sense believes to be true.

"Your life is dear; for all that life can rate as worthy of life has in you estimate. You have everything that we consider valuable in life: youth, beauty, wisdom, courage, all that happiness and the prime of youth can happy call.

"Your risking these things in your bet that you can cure me intimates to me that either you have infinite medical skill or you are monstrously desperate.

"Sweet practitioner of the medical art, your medicine I will try — your medicine that administers your own death if I die."

Helena said, "If you are not cured in one or two days, or if I come up short in giving you the healthful properties of which I spoke, unpitied let me die a well-deserved death. If I don't help you, death's my fee, but if I do help you, what do you promise me?"

"Make your demand," the King said. "Tell me what you want."

"But will you give me what I ask?" Helena asked.

"Yes, I swear by my scepter and my hopes of Heaven," the King replied.

Helena said, "Then you shall give me with your Kingly hand what husband in your power I will command. You will give me whatever man to marry I chose from among those men you have the power to marry off. Exempted be from me the arrogance to choose from forth the royal blood of France — I will not choose to marry French royalty. I will not insist that my low and humble name be allowed to propagate with any branch or image of your state. But such a one, your vassal, whom I know it is allowed for me to ask for, I want you to bestow on me."

Bertram was the King's ward. As Bertram's guardian, the King had the right to arrange a marriage for him to anyone of equal rank; however, Helena was not of equal rank to Bertram. Still, Bertram was not so high ranking that he was French royalty.

"Here is my hand," the King said. "The promises observed — that is, once you have done what you have promised — your will by my performance shall be served: You will get what you ask for. So make the choice in your own time, for I, who am now resolved to be your patient, on you continually rely.

"More should I question you, and more I must, although more to know could not be more to trust. I trust you completely without knowing more about you.

"I would like to know from whence you came and how you were escorted here, but go now and rest with an unquestioned welcome and undoubted blessing."

He shouted for an attendant, "Give me some help here, ho!"

Then he said to Helena, "If you proceed as high as was promised by your word, my deed shall match your deed."

The Countess was talking to her Fool in the Count of Rousillon's palace. She wanted the Fool to carry a letter to the French King's court and wanted to know if the Fool would behave himself there.

"Come on, sir," she said. "I shall now make you show the height of your upbringing. I will test you to see what kind of man you are."

"I will show myself highly fed and lowly taught. I know my business is only to the court," the Fool replied.

"Better fed than taught" was a phrase said about the spoiled children of rich people. Such children were well born but badly disciplined. They were well fed but had not learned good manners. The Fool was criticizing the court, which according to the Fool did not value gentle nurture and a good upbringing.

The Fool was also denigrating the court by saying that his business was "only" to the court. If his business was only to the court, it must not be important business.

"Only to the court!" the Countess said. "Why, what place do you consider special, when you dismiss the court with such contempt? Only to the court!"

"Truly, madam, if God has lent a man any manners, he may easily pull it off and be a success at court," the Fool said, continuing his criticism of the court. "He who cannot make a leg kneel, put off his cap, or kiss his hand and say nothing has neither leg, cap, hands, nor lip, and indeed such a fellow, to say precisely, were not for the court."

According to the Fool, to be a success at court, all one had to do was to engage in some showy displays of etiquette.

The Fool continued, "But as for me, I have an answer that will serve all men."

"By the Virgin Mary," the Countess said, "that's a bountiful answer if it fits all questions."

"It is like a barber's chair that fits all buttocks: the skinny buttocks, the squat buttocks, the muscular buttocks, or any other buttocks," the Fool said.

"Will your answer serve as an appropriate answer to all questions?" the Countess asked.

"It will be as appropriate as ten groats — ten four-penny coins — is for the hand of an attorney," the Fool said.

Ten groats was the usual fee for an attorney's services.

The Fool continued, "It will be as appropriate as your French crown for your taffeta punk."

A taffeta punk was a prostitute dressed in showy taffeta clothing. A French crown was a piece of money; it also referred to the baldness caused by syphilis, which was known as the French disease. In other words, a French crown was both what a prostitute received for her services and what she gave to those who used her services.

The Fool continued, "It will be as appropriate as Tib's rush for Tom's forefinger."

"Tib" and "Tom" were names for "lass" and "lad." Country girls would make rings out of rushes and give them to boyfriends. Country girls would also rush to their boyfriends, or to parts of their boyfriends. A forefinger would fit into a ring, and a forefinger or a "forefinger" would fit into another kind of hole.

The Fool continued, "It will be as appropriate as a pancake for Shrove Tuesday or a morris for May Day."

Pancakes were often served on Shrove Tuesday, the day before Lent began. Morris dances were performed on May Day.

The Fool continued, "It will be as appropriate as the nail is to its hole, the cuckold to his horn, as a scolding quean — hussy — to a wrangling knave, as the nun's lip to the friar's mouth, and as the pudding to its skin."

The Fool was distorting a well-known proverb: "As fit as a pudding for a friar's mouth."

A pudding is a sausage.

The Countess asked, "Do you have, I say, an answer of such fitness for all questions?"

"From below your Duke to beneath your constable, it will fit any question," the Fool said.

His answer would fit any question the way a barber's chair would fit any set of buttocks, including those of a Duke and those of a constable.

"It must be an answer of very monstrous size that must fit all demands," the Countess said.

"It's nothing but a trifle, indeed, if the learned would speak the truth about it," the Fool replied. "Here it is, and all that belongs to it. Ask me if I am a courtier: It shall do you no harm to learn."

The Countess said, "To be young again, if only we could."

It is good not to be so old that one cannot learn.

She continued, "I will be a fool in questioning you, hoping to become wiser by your answer. I ask you, sir, are you a courtier?"

"Oh, Lord, sir!" the Fool said. This was his all-purpose answer to any question. These words were used at court to avoid answering questions. These words could also be used to reply to statements. With different inflections, the meaning of the three-word answer could vary.

The Fool continued, "There's a simple putting off — disposing of — the question. More, more, give me a hundred questions or conversational tidbits."

"Sir, I am a poor friend of yours, who loves you," the Countess said.

"Oh, Lord, sir!" the Fool said. "Let your words come thickly, thickly — don't spare me."

"I think, sir, you can eat none of this simple food."

"Oh, Lord, sir!" the Fool said. "Put me to it! Challenge me! I want you to!"

"You were recently whipped, sir, I think," the Countess said.

"Oh, Lord, sir! Don't spare me!" the Fool said.

This is not the thing to say while being whipped.

The Countess said, "Do you cry, 'Oh, Lord, sir!' at your whipping, and 'Don't spare me?' Indeed, your 'Oh, Lord, sir!' is very sequent to your whipping. You would answer very well to a whipping, if you were but bound to it."

She was engaging in wordplay. "Answer to" meant both "reply to" and "suffer the consequences of." "Bound to it" meant both "obliged to reply" and "bound to the whipping post."

"I never had worse luck in my life in my 'Oh, Lord, sir!' answer," the Fool said. "I see things may serve well for a long time, but not serve well forever."

"I see that I am playing the noble housewife who has the time to entertain herself so merrily with a Fool," the Countess said.

In other words, she was wasting time.

"Oh, Lord, sir!" the Fool said. "Why, there my answer serves well again."

"Put an end, sir, to your foolish business," the Countess said.

She gave the Fool a letter and said, "Give this to Helen in Paris and urge her to write an immediate answer back. Commend me to my kinsmen and my son. This is not much."

"Not too much commendation to them?" the Fool asked.

"Not too much work for you to do," the Countess replied. "Do you understand me?"

In his answer, the Fool understood the word "understood" to have a bawdy meaning. A "stand" is an "erection"; erections can be fruitful if they result in the birth of a child.

"I understand you most fruitfully," the Fool replied. "I am there before my legs."

Because of his erection, part of the Fool would be in Paris before his legs arrived there.

"Hasten back home again," the Countess said.

— 2.3 —

Bertram, Lafeu, and Parolles spoke together in a room in the French King's palace. They were talking about the French King's miraculous recovery from his deadly illness. Lafeu was holding a printed ballad about the King's miraculous recovery.

Lafeu said, "They say miracles are past, and we have our philosophical persons to make commonplace and familiar, things that are supernatural and without a natural cause. Hence it is that we make trifles of terrors, barricading ourselves with seeming knowledge, when we should submit ourselves to fear of the unknown."

Protestants felt that the age of miracles was past, while Catholics believed that miracles were still possible in the latter — modern — age.

"Why, it is the rarest theme of wonder that has shot out in our latter times," Parolles said.

"And so it is," Bertram said.

Lafeu said, "To be given up by the physicians —"

Parolles interrupted, "So I say."

"— physicians who follow Galen and physicians who follow Paracelsus," Lafeu said.

Galen was an ancient physician, while Paracelsus was a modern physician.

Parolles interrupted, "So I say."

Lafeu said, "Of all the learned and accredited practitioners —"

Parolles interrupted, "Right! So I say."

Lafeu said, "Who said that the King was incurable —"

Parolles interrupted, "Why, there it is. So say I, too."

Lafeu said, "Who said that the King could not be helped —"

Parolles interrupted, "Right; as it were, a man assured of a —"

Lafeu interrupted, "— uncertain life, and sure death."

Parolles said, "Right, you say well; so would I have said."

"I may truly say," Lafeu said, "it is a novelty to the world."

"It is, indeed," Parolles said. "If you will have it in showing, you shall read it in — what do you call it there?"

Lafeu read out loud the title of the printed ballad: "A Showing of a Heavenly Effect in an Earthly Actor."

"That's it," Parolles said. "I would have said the very same."

Lafeu said, "Why, a dolphin is not more vigorous than the King now. By my word, I speak in respect —"

Parolles said, "It is strange, it is very strange, that is the brief and the tedious of it."

Parolles was using highfalutin' language. He used "the brief and the tedious" rather than "the long and the short." Next he would use "facinerious" rather than "extremely wicked."

He continued, "And he's of a most facinerious spirit who will not acknowledge it to be the —"

Lafeu interrupted, "— very hand of Heaven."

"Yes, so I say," Parolles said.

Lafeu said, "In a most weak —"

Parolles interrupted, "— and debile, aka feeble, agent, great power, great transcendence, which should, indeed, give us a further use to be made than alone the recovery of the King, as to be —"

Lafeu interrupted, "— generally thankful."

"That's what I was going to say," Parolles said. "You said it well. Here comes the King."

The King, Helena, and some attendants entered the room.

Lafeu said, "The King is *lustig*, aka frolicsome, as the German says. I'll like a maiden all the better, while I have a tooth in my head. Why, the King's able to lead her in the quick-stepping, lively dance known as the *coranto*."

Parolles said, "*Mort du vinaigre*! Isn't this Helen?"

He was so shocked that he mangled his French and said something that could possibly be translated as "Death of vinegar!"

"By God, I think so," Lafeu said. He, of course, knew that she was Helena, but he had become aware that Parolles was a fool and so he was not inclined to be helpful to him.

The King ordered an attendant, "Go, call before me all the lords in the court."

He said to Helena, "Sit, my preserver, by your patient's side, and with this healthy hand, whose banished sense you have called back from the exile that is death, a second time receive the confirmation of my promised gift, which but awaits your naming. You will now choose your husband."

Four lords entered the room. These were lords who were wards of the King, who had the right to marry them to a woman of an equal social status. Bertram joined the four lords.

The King said to Helena, "Fair maiden, look at these lords. This youthful parcel of noble bachelors stands at my bestowing, over whom I have the power to use both sovereign power and father's voice. Make your free choice among these men. You have power to choose, and they have no power to reject you. Choose freely."

Helena said to the lords, "To each of you may one fair and virtuous mistress fall, when the god of Love pleases! May each of you get a beautiful and virtuous woman to marry! To each of you, but one!"

She was being modest. She wanted one lord — Bertram — to marry her, and she wanted to avoid the boast that she was beautiful and virtuous. She would claim that she was virtuous, but she was unwilling to claim that she was also beautiful. Others, however, were to claim that she was both beautiful and virtuous.

Lafeu said, "I would give my bay horse Curtal, so named because of his docked tail, and his trappings and harness, for my teeth to be no more broken than these boys' and for my beard to be as little written on my face."

The King said to Helena, "Look them over well. Not one of those young lords lacks a noble father."

Helena stood up and said to the lords, "Gentlemen, Heaven has through me restored the King to health."

The lords replied, "We understand it, and we thank Heaven for you."

She said, "I am a simple maiden, and therein wealthiest in that I avow I truly am a maiden. If it pleases your majesty, I have done already."

She already knew her choice.

She continued, "The blushes in my cheeks thus whisper to me, 'We blush that you should choose, but if you are refused, let the pallor of death sit on your cheek forever. We'll never come there again.'"

The King said, "Make your choice and see what happens. Whoever shuns your love shuns all his love in me."

Helena said, "Now, Diana, virgin goddess, from your altar do I fly, and to imperial Love, that god most high, do my sighs stream."

She moved to the first lord and said, "Sir, will you hear my suit?"

The first lord said, "Yes, and I will grant it."

Helena wanted to marry Bertram, so this answer did not suit her.

"Thanks, sir," she said. "All the rest is mute."

In other words, she would not make her suit to him.

She moved to the next lord.

Lafeu said, "By my life, I swear that I would rather be in this choice than throw on and endure ames-ace — worthless ecclesiastical clothing."

He was saying that it was better to be in the world, get married, and have sex with Helena than to be a celibate member of the clergy.

"Amice," sometimes spelled in this culture as "ames," is ecclesiastical clothing; "ace" figuratively means "worthless."

By the way, according to the *Oxford English Dictionary*, in this culture the word "amice" was spelled in many ways: "amyse," "amis(e," "ames," "amyss(e," "amys(e," "amias," "ammess," and "amyce," as well as "amice."

Helena said to the second lord, whose admiration of her was evident in his eyes, "The honor, sir, that flames in your fair eyes, before I speak, too threateningly replies to my question: 'Sir, will you hear my suit?'"

The threat was that the lord would ask Helena to marry him. Any of the four lords would be happy to honor and marry her.

Helena continued, "May Love make your fortunes twenty times above her — me — who so wishes such fortune for you, and may Love make your fortunes twenty times above her humble love!"

The second lord said, "I wish no better than you, if you please."

"Receive my wish for you, which I hope that great Love will grant!" Helena said. "And so, I take my leave of you."

Lafeu was too far away to hear what was being said. He could see Helena going from lord to lord and he thought that the lords were rejecting her, rather than that she was rejecting the lords.

"Do they all reject her?" Lafeu said. "If they were sons of mine, I'd have them whipped, or I would send them to the Turks to make eunuchs of."

Helena said to the third lord, "Be not afraid that I your hand should take. I'll never do you wrong for your own sake. Blessing upon your vows! And in your bed may you find fairer fortune, if you ever wed!"

"These boys are boys of ice," Lafeu complained. "None of them will marry her. Surely, they are bastards to the English; the French never begot them."

Helena said to the fourth lord, "You are too young, too happy, and too good to make yourself a son out of my blood."

"Fair one, I think not so," the fourth lord replied. "I would be happy if you were the mother of my son."

Lafeu said, referring to Bertram, "There's one grape yet; I am sure your father drank wine, and we all know that good wine makes good blood, but if you are not an ass, I am a fourteen-year-old youth. I have known you already, and I know that you are an ass."

Why would he think that Bertram is an ass? Because Bertram associated with Parolles, who was an ass, as shown by the recent conversation between Parolles and Lafeu. Also, Bertram had been rude while Lafeu was visiting Rousillon.

Helena said to Bertram, "I dare not say I take you, but I give myself and my service, for as long as I live, to your guiding power."

She said to the King, "This is the man I choose to marry."

The King said, "Why, then, young Bertram, take her; she's your wife."

"My wife, my liege!" Bertram said. "I shall entreat your highness in such a business to give me leave to use the help of my own eyes. When it comes to taking a wife, let me make my own choice."

"Don't you know, Bertram, what she has done for me?" the King asked.

"Yes, my good lord," Bertram replied, "but I never hope to know why I should marry her."

"You know that she has raised me from my sickbed," the King said.

"But does it follow, my lord, that I must bring myself down to pay for your raising up?" Bertram asked. "I know her well. She had her upbringing at my father's charge. That a poor physician's daughter should be my wife! My disdain and contempt for her would corrupt and ruin me forever!"

The King said, "It is only the title of 'poor physician's daughter' that you disdain in her, and I can build up her title. It is strange that our veins' blood, poured all together in a basin, would quite confound making any distinction of color, weight, and heat, yet our blood — lineage and ancestral descent — make so mighty differences.

"If she is all that is virtuous, except for that title that you dislike, the title and name of 'poor physician's daughter,' then you dislike virtue because of the name, but don't do that.

"From the lowest place when virtuous things proceed, the place is dignified by the doer's deed. Where great additions — titles and names — swell, and virtue does not swell, it is a dropsied, puffed-up honor.

"Good alone is good without a name. Vileness is vile without a name.

"The property should be valued by what it is, not by the title.

"Helen is young, wise, and fair; she inherited these things from nature, and these things breed honor.

"True honor scorns what calls itself honorable as a result of ancestry and is not like the real thing, which is honorable as a result of honorable behavior.

"The mere word 'honor' is a slave that appears and is debauched on every tomb, on every grave it is a lying trophy, and as often it is dumb and silent where dust and damned oblivion is the tomb of honored bones indeed. The word 'honor' is often given to those deceased who do not deserve it and as often withheld from those deceased who do deserve it.

"What should now be said? If you can like this creature of God as a maiden, I can create the rest. Virtue and she herself are her own dower; honor and wealth are her dower from me."

"I cannot love her, nor will I strive to love her," Bertram said.

"You wrong yourself, if you should strive to make your own choice," the King said.

If Bertram insisted on choosing his own wife, he would get on the King's bad side, and that was not wise.

Helena, who did not want Bertram to be hurt, said to the King, "That you are well restored to health, my lord, I'm glad. Let the rest go. I need no reward for what I did."

"My honor's at the stake," the King said.

He was referring to bear-baiting, in which a bear was tied to a stake and then tormented by dogs.

The King added, "To defeat this challenge to my honor, I must produce and use my power."

He said to Bertram, using the contemptuous insult "boy," "Here, take her hand, proud and scornful boy, unworthy of this good gift. You in vile misprision — disdain — shackle up my love and her desert."

In addition to meaning "disdain," the word "misprision" punned on "false imprisonment."

The King continued, "You put her in a scale and weigh her against yourself and find her lacking. You cannot dream that we, placing ourselves in her scale that is deficient compared to yours, shall outweigh you so much that your scale will fly up to the crossbeam. You will not know that we have the power to plant your honor where we please to have it grow.

"Check your contempt. Obey our will, which labors for your good. Don't believe your disdain, but immediately do your own fortunes that obedient right that both your duty to us owes and our power claims, or I will throw you from my care forever into the staggering and careless lapse of youth and ignorance. I will let loose both my revenge and hate upon you, in the name of justice, without pity in any form.

"Speak; give me your answer."

The King really did have the power he claimed. He would be a formidable enemy.

Bertram backed off: "Give me pardon, my gracious lord, for I submit my fancy and affection to your eyes. When I consider what creation of greatness and what share of honor flies where you bid it, I find that she, who recently was in my nobler thoughts most base, is now praised by the King. She, being ennobled by such praise, is as if she were born so noble."

"Take her by the hand, and tell her she is yours," the King ordered.

This action, called a handfasting, in this society was itself a legal contract of marriage, although the church also wanted a religious marriage ceremony. A marriage feast usually soon followed the marriage ceremony.

The King continued, "I promise to Helena a counterweight: I cannot raise her birth as high as yours, but I will make her wealth more than yours."

"I take her hand," Bertram said, doing so.

The King said, "Good fortune and the favor of the King smile upon this contract of marriage. The religious marriage ceremony shall follow quickly upon my royal command, which I now give: It will be performed tonight.

"The solemnizing marriage feast shall wait for a time, until friends who are absent now can arrive and share in the feast.

"As you love her, so is your love to me. If your love for her is religious, holy, and true, it is good; if it is not religious, holy, and true, it errs."

Everyone exited except for Lafeu and Parolles, who were a short distance apart.

Lafeu walked over to Parolles and asked him, "Did you hear that, monsieur? I would like a word with you."

"What is your pleasure, sir? What do you want?"

"Your lord and master did well to make his recantation," Lafeu said.

The word "recantation" is interesting. A religious heretic can recant his or her heresy.

Parolles took umbrage, both to Lafeu's use of the word "recantation" and to Bertram being called his "lord and master." He regarded himself as Bertram's equal.

"Recantation! My lord! My master!" Parolles said.

"Yes," Lafeu replied. "Aren't the sounds I speak a language?"

"They are a very harsh language," Parolles replied, "and not to be understood without bloodshed following. My master!"

Lafeu asked, "Are you companion to the Count Rousillon?"

The word "companion" meant both "rascal" and "associate."

"To any Count, to all Counts, to what is man," Parolles replied.

Parolles was claiming to be on equal terms with all men. Lafeu rejected this because he had a low opinion of Parolles and considered him to be Bertram's servant.

Lafeu said, "To what is Count's manservant. Count's master is of another style."

Count Rousillon's master was the King of France. Lafeu was saying that Parolles was the manservant of a Count, but he, Lafeu, knew the Count's master well.

"You are too old for me to fight, sir," Parolles said. "Let it satisfy you, you are too old."

Parolles was saying that he would fight Lafeu because of Lafeu's insults, except that Lafeu was too old to fight.

"I must tell you, sirrah, that I am a man," Lafeu said. "That is a title that you will not have even when you are old."

"What I can do only too well, I dare not do," Parolles said. "I could easily beat you, but because of your age, I will not."

Lafeu said, "I did think you, for the time it takes to eat two meals, to be a pretty wise fellow. You made tolerable conversation about your travels. Your conversation might pass you off as an intelligent person, yet the numerous showy military sashes and banners you wear in manifold ways dissuaded me from believing you to be a vessel of very much capacity. You wear so many military sashes and banners that you look like a ship flying many flags.

"I have now found you out, and I know what you are, which isn't much. When I lose you again, I won't care. Yet you are good for nothing but taking up; and you are scarcely worth taking up."

"Taking up" has such meanings as "picking up," "arresting," and "rebuking."

"If you had not the privilege of old age upon you —" Parolles began.

"Do not plunge yourself too far in anger, lest you hasten your trial," Lafeu said, referring to a trial by combat. "If this trial should happen — may the Lord have mercy on you for the hen — woman — you are!

"So, my good window of lattice, fare you well. Your window I need not open, for I look through you."

Lafeu was saying that Parolles was common; common alehouses had latticework windows. His many sashes also made him look like a latticework window.

Lafeu said, "Give me your hand."

He was willing to depart with a handshake; it wasn't as if he and Parolles were going to fight — ever. A trial by combat would never happen. Lafeu was too old to fight, and Parolles was too cowardly to fight. And trials by combat were reserved for such crimes as treason.

Parolles still took umbrage: "My lord, you give me most egregious indignity. You have egregiously insulted me!"

"Yes, I have, and with all my heart; and you are worthy of every insult."

"I have not, my lord, deserved these insults," Parolles replied.

"Yes, indeed, you have deserved every last bit of these insults, and I will not take back even a tiny bit of one of them."

"Well, I shall be wiser," Parolles said.

He meant that he would not talk to Lafeu in the future, but Lafeu took the meaning literally.

"Be wiser as soon as you can," Lafeu said, "for you have to taste a quantity of your foolishness before you grow wise. If ever you are bound in your sashes and banners and beaten, you shall find out what it is to be proud of your bondage — your sashes and banners that you bind to your body.

"I desire to continue my acquaintance with you, or rather my knowledge of you, so that I may say in the default that he is — you are — a man I know."

When Parolles' character was weighed, he would be found lacking — he would be in default.

"My lord, you do me most insupportable vexation," Parolles said.

"I wish the vexations were hell-pains for your sake, and I wish my poor doing would be eternal. If I had the power, I would damn you to hell — that is what I would do. For some kinds of doing, I — old man that I am — am past doing, and now I will pass by you. My old age still allows me to do that motion."

Lafeu exited.

Alone, Parolles said to himself, "Well, you have a son who shall take this disgrace off me. I will fight him."

Actually, Parolles was in no danger of actually getting in a fight; he knew that Lafeu had no son, only a daughter.

He continued, "Scurvy, old, filthy, scurvy lord! Well, I must be patient; there is no fettering of authority. I'll beat him, by my life, if I can meet him on any suitable and convenient occasion, and I would beat him even if he were double and double a lord. I'll have no more pity on his old age than I would on — I'll beat him, if I could but meet him again."

Lafeu returned. Parolles had his chance. Parolles did not take his chance.

Lafeu said, "Sirrah, your lord and master is married; there's news for you: You have a new mistress."

"I most unfeignedly, genuinely, and sincerely beseech your lordship to make some reservation of your wrongs," Parolles said. "Do not display them. Bertram is my good lord. He Whom I serve above is my master."

Actually, one meaning of "lord" is "master."

"Who? God?"

"Yes, sir."

"The Devil is the being who is your master," Lafeu said to the fancily dressed Parolles. "Why do you garter up your arms in this fashion? People wear garters on their legs. Do you make stockings out of your sleeves? Do other servants do so? Since you do this, it would be best for you to set your lower part where your nose stands — let your penis be placed where your nose is.

"By my honor, I swear that if I were only two hours younger, I would beat you. I think that you are a general offence, and every man should beat you. I think you were created so that men could get exercise by beating you."

"This is hard and undeserved treatment, my lord," Parolles said.

"That is bull, sir. You were beaten in Italy for picking a kernel out of a pomegranate — petty theft," Lafeu said. "You are a vagabond and no true traveller; you travel without the necessary legal documents. You are saucier with lords and honorable personages than the warrant of your birth and virtue gives you heraldry. You are not worth another word, else I would call you 'knave.' I leave you."

He exited.

Parolles said to himself, "Good, very good; it is so then. That's the way it stands between us. Good, very good. Let it be concealed awhile."

Bertram entered the room.

He said, "I am ruined and forfeited to cares and worries forever!"

"What's the matter, sweet heart?" Parolles asked, trying to get Bertram's attention.

"Although before the solemn priest I have sworn and I have married her, I will not bed her," Bertram said.

"What? What's the matter, sweet heart?" Parolles asked again.

"Oh, my Parolles, they have married me! I'll go to the Tuscan wars, and never bed her."

"France is a dog hole, and it no longer deserves the tread of a man's foot. Let's go to the wars!"

"There's a letter from my mother," Bertram said. "What the content is, I don't know yet."

"Yes, that should be known," Parolles said. "To the wars, my boy, to the wars! He wears his honor in a box — vagina — unseen, who hugs his kicky-wicky wife here at home, expending his manly marrow — his semen —

while in her arms, marrow that should sustain the bound and high jump of Mars' fiery steed."

Possibly, a kicky-wicky wife is one who kicks — humps — when her husband's wick — penis — is inside her.

Parolles continued, "Compared to other regions, France is a stable; we who dwell in it are jades, aka broken-down horses. Therefore, to the war!"

"It shall be so," Bertram said. "I'll send Helena, my wife, to my house, acquaint my mother with my hatred of her, and tell my mother for what reason I am fled. I will write to the King that which I dare not speak to him; his recent gift to me shall equip me so that I can fight on those Italian battlefields where noble fellows strike blows. War is no strife when compared to the dark, unhappy house and the detested wife."

"Will this *capriccio* hold in you?" Parolles asked. "Are you sure?"

"*Capriccio*" is Italian for "caprice" or "whim."

"Go with me to my chamber, and advise me," Bertram said. "I'll send her immediately away. Tomorrow I'll go to the wars, and she will go to her single sorrow."

"Why, these balls rebound; there's noise in it. It is hard," Parolles said.

Using tennis as a metaphor, Parolles was saying that Bertram was playing the game as it ought to be played, hitting the ball hard and making the tennis ball bounce.

Parolles added, "A young man married is a man who's marred."

A proverb stated, "Marrying is marring."

Parolles continued, "Therefore, let's go away and bravely leave her; let's go. The King has done you wrong, but hush, it is so."

— 2.4 —

Helena and the Fool, who had arrived from the Count of Rousillon's palace with a letter for her, spoke together in a room of the French King's palace.

Helena, who had read the letter, said, "My mother greets me kindly; is she well?"

The Countess of Rousillon, Bertram's mother, was now Helena's mother-in-law.

"She is not well; but yet she has her health," the Fool said. "She's very merry, but yet she is not well, but thanks be given, she's very well and wants nothing in the world, but yet she is not well."

The Fool was punning on these two meanings of "well": 1) in good health, and 2) in Heaven. A proverb stated, "He is well since he is in Heaven."

"If she is very well, what is ailing her, so that she's not very well?" Helena asked.

"Truly, she's very well indeed, but for two things," the Fool said.

"What two things?"

"One, that she's not in Heaven, whither may God send her quickly! The other is that she's on Earth, from whence may God send her quickly!"

Parolles entered the room.

"Bless you, my fortunate lady!" he said to Helena.

"I hope, sir, I have your good will to have my own good fortunes," Helena replied.

"You had my prayers to lead them on, and to keep them on, you have my prayers still," Parolles said.

He then asked the Fool, "Oh, my knave, how does my old lady?"

Parolles had pronounced "does" much like the way many people pronounce "dies." This was common in this society.

"Provided that you inherited her wrinkles and I her money, I wish she did as you say," the Fool replied.

"Why, I say nothing," Parolles said.

"Indeed, then you are the wiser man, for many a man's tongue shakes out his master's undoing. Often, men say things that ruin the men's masters. To say nothing, to do nothing, to know nothing, and to have nothing is to be a great part of your entitlement, which is within a very little of nothing — and that is what you will inherit from her."

"Go away!" Parolles said. "You are a knave."

"You should have said, sir, before a knave you are a knave," the Fool said. "That is, you should have said, sir, that before me you are a knave. This would have been the truth, sir."

"Before me" was an oath, and it also meant "physically here before me." The Fool was calling Parolles a knave.

"Go on, you are a witty fool," Parolles said. "I have found you out."

"Did you find me in yourself, sir? Or were you taught to find me?" the Fool asked.

"Did you find me in yourself, sir?" had a double meaning: 1) "Did you find me by yourself?" and 2) "Did you find foolery in yourself?"

The Fool already knew the answer to the question: Parolles was very much a fool.

The Fool said, "The search, sir, was profitable, and much fool may you find in you, even to the world's pleasure and the increase of laughter."

"You are a good knave, indeed, and you are well fed," Parolles said, alluding to the saying "Better fed than taught."

Parolles then said to Helena, "Madam, my lord will go away tonight; a very serious business calls on him to take action. The great prerogative and rite of love, aka the marriage consummation, which as your due the present time claims, he does acknowledge, but he puts it off due to a compelled restraint. He will not consummate the marriage yet. The lack of the consummation, and its delay, is strewn with sweet-scented flowers, which distil now into a sweet-smelling liquid in the curbed time, to make the coming hour overflow with joy and pleasure drown the brim. The delay will increase anticipation, which will increase the enjoyment of the consummation of your marriage."

"What else is my husband's will?" Helena asked.

"That you will take your immediate leave of the King and say that your leaving so quickly is your own idea and that you have a good reason for this haste," Parolles said. "Make up whatever excuse you think may make your immediate departure plausible and necessary."

"What more does he command?"

"That, having obtained permission from the King for your immediate departure, you immediately go to him and find out his further pleasure."

"In everything I wait upon his will," Helena said. "I am an obedient wife."

In this culture, good wives were obedient wives.

"I shall report it so to him," Parolles said.

"Please do," Helena said.

Parolles exited.

Helena said to the Fool, "Come, sirrah."

They exited.

— 2.5 —

Lafeu and Bertram spoke together about Parolles in a room in the French King's palace.

Lafeu said, "But I hope your lordship does not think that he is a soldier."

"Yes, I do, my lord, and of a very valiant proven character," Bertram replied.

"He himself has told you that," Lafeu said.

"Yes, but I also have heard it from other warranted and legitimate testimony."

"Then my compass dial does not go true," Lafeu said. "It does not point north. I mistook this lark for a bunting. I mistook a good man for a poor man."

"I do assure you, my lord, that he is very great in knowledge and accordingly valiant," Bertram said.

"I have then sinned against his experience and transgressed against his valor," Lafeu said, "and my state that way is dangerous, since I cannot yet find in my heart to repent. My soul is in danger of damnation because of the way I have misjudged him."

He looked up, saw Parolles entering the room, and said, "Here he comes. Please, make us friends; I will pursue the friendship."

Parolles walked over to Bertram and said, "These things shall be done, sir."

Parolles was flashily dressed, as always, and Lafeu's resolution — if it really was a resolution — to be friends with him vanished. He decided that if he had made a mistake about Parolles' character, it was thinking that Parolles' character was better than it actually was; in other words, Parolles was a worse man than Lafeu had previously thought him to be. To be honest, Lafeu also did not think that Bertram was nearly as good a man as he ought to be. Lafeu may not have meant it when he said that he was wrong about Parolles and wanted to be reconciled to him. In contrast to Parolles, Bertram was high ranking, and Lafeu would not criticize him openly.

Lafeu said to Bertram about Parolles, "Please, sir, tell me who's his tailor? Who made this mannequin?"

He was pretending that Parolles was a tailor-made man — that a tailor had made his clothes, and that his clothes made the man; in other words, Parolles' clothes were better than he himself was. The clothes were military, but Parolles was in no way a military man.

"Sir?" Parolles said.

Pretending that "Sir" was the name of the tailor, Lafeu said, "Oh, I know him well. I do, sir. He, sir, is a good workman, a very good tailor."

The implication was Parolles was a very good mannequin.

Bertram asked Parolles, "Is Helena going to the King?"

"She is."

"Will she leave tonight?"

"Yes, just as you want her to," Parolles answered.

Bertram said, "I have written my letters, put my valuables in a casket, and given orders for our horses. Tonight, when I should take possession of the bride, I will end my marriage before I begin it."

Lafeu said while looking straight at Parolles, "A good traveller is something good at the latter end of a dinner because he can tell tales, but a traveller who lies three thirds — all! — of the time and uses a known truth to pass a thousand false nothings with, should be once heard and thrice beaten."

He then said to Bertram, "May God save you, Captain."

Bertram said to Parolles, "Is there any unkindness between my lord and you, monsieur?"

Parolles replied, "I don't know how I have deserved to run into my lord's displeasure."

In his reply, Lafeu took "run into" as "rush headlong into": "You have made shift to run into it, boots and spurs and all, like the clown who leaped into the custard at a festival, and out of it you'll run again, rather than suffer question for your residence."

Vagabonds were questioned about their residence; they could be whipped for being where they ought not to be and for traveling without the legal documents needed for traveling.

"It may be you have mistaken him, my lord," Bertram said.

Bertram used the word "mistaken" to mean "made a mistake about his character," but in his reply Lafeu used it to mean "take for evil." He also used the word "take" to mean "apprehend."

"And I shall do so always, even if I were to take him at his prayers," Lafeu said to Bertram. "Fare you well, my lord; and believe this of me, there can be no kernel in this light nut; the soul of this man is his clothes. Don't trust him when it comes to important matters. I have kept such creatures as pets, and I know their natures."

He then said to Parolles, "Farewell, monsieur. I have spoken better of you than you have or ever will deserve at my hand, but we must do good against evil."

Lafeu exited.

"He is an idle, foolish, stupid lord, I swear," Parolles said.

"I think so," Bertram replied, agreeing with his companion, but he sounded doubtful.

Parolles heard the doubt in his voice.

"Why, don't you know him?" Parolles asked. "Haven't you figured out what his real character is yet?"

"Yes, I do know him well, and common speech gives him a worthy reputation," Bertram said.

Helena, accompanied by an attendant, entered the room, and as she walked over to them, Bertram said to Parolles, "Here comes my ball and chain."

Helena said to Bertram, "I have done, sir, what I was commanded to do by you. I have spoken with the King and have procured his leave for an immediate departure, but he wants to have some private conversation with you."

"I shall obey his will," Bertram said. "You must not marvel, Helen, at my course of action, which seems inappropriate to the time and which does not fulfill the ministration and required office on my particular role as your husband. At this time I am not fulfilling my obligations as a husband. I was not prepared for such a business as marriage; therefore, I am very much unsettled. This drives me to entreat you to immediately make your way home. I prefer that you wonder why rather than that you ask me why I entreat you to do this, for my reasons are better than they seem and my arrangements have in them a need greater than shows itself at first sight to you who don't know them."

He handed her a letter and said, "Give this to my mother. It will be two days before I shall see you, so I leave you to your wisdom."

"Sir, I can say nothing, except that I am your most obedient servant," Helena said.

In this culture, good wives were obedient wives.

"Come, come, no more of that," Bertram said.

"And I always shall with true observance seek to increase that wherein toward me my homely stars have failed to equal my great fortune," Helena said.

Helena's "homely stars" were planets whose astrological influence had doomed her to a lowly birth. Her "great fortune" was being married to Bertram, as well as the fortune the King was giving to her. Helena was saying that she would do all she could to make up for her lowly birth. Bertram was refusing to sleep with her, and she knew that it was because of her birth.

"Let that go," Bertram said. "My haste is very great. Farewell. Hurry home."

"Please, sir, I beg your pardon," Helena said.

"Well, what do you want to say to me?"

"I am not worthy of the wealth I own, nor do I dare to say it is mine, and yet it is," Helena said. "But, like a timid thief, I most gladly would steal what law does vouch to be my own."

"What would you have?" Bertram asked.

"Something; and scarcely so much," Helena said. "Nothing, indeed. I would not tell you what I want, my lord. But yes, I will, indeed: Strangers and foes part, and do not kiss."

She was asking for a kiss as they parted from each other.

"Please, don't stay here, but hasten to your horse," Bertram said.

He was unwilling to kiss her.

"I shall not break your bidding, my good lord," Helena said. "I will do as you say."

She asked her attendant, "Where are my other men, monsieur?"

Then Helena said to Bertram, "Farewell."

Helena exited; she and her attendant talked quietly.

Bertram said quietly after her departing form, "Go toward home, where I will never come while I can shake my sword or hear the drum."

He said to Parolles, "Let's go, and prepare for our flight."

Parolles replied, "Bravely, *coragio*!"

"*Coragio*" is Italian for "courage."

CHAPTER 3

— 3.1 —

The Duke of Florence talked with two French lords in a room in his palace in Florence. Some attendants and soldiers were present.

The Duke of Florence said, "So now from point to point and in every particular you have heard the fundamental reasons for and causes of this war, the deciding of which has let forth much blood and thirsts to let forth much more blood."

The first French lord said, "Holy seems the quarrel upon your grace's part, but black and fearful upon the part of the opposer."

"Therefore we marvel much that our cousin, aka fellow-sovereign, the King of France, would in so just a business shut his bosom against our prayers for aid."

The second French lord replied, "My good lord, the reasons and explanations of our government I cannot comment on, because I am a common man and an outsider to the great doings of a council of state. I can only imperfectly guess at what happens in such proceedings, and therefore I dare not say what I think about them, since I have found myself in my uncertain guesses to be mistaken as often as I guessed."

"Let it be as the King of France wants," the Duke of Florence said.

The first French lord said, "But I am sure the younger men of our nation, who grow ill because of their ease, will day by day come here for medical help. The bloodletting of the war will heal them."

In this society, bleeding was often used to medically treat a patient.

The Duke of Florence said, "Welcome they shall be, and all the honors that can fly from us shall on them settle. You know your places well; when better places become available, they become available for your advantage. You shall have those places. Tomorrow we go to the battlefield."

The Countess of Rousillon and the Fool spoke together in the Count of Rousillon's palace.

The Countess said, "It has all happened as I would have had it, except that he has not come along with her."

"Truly," the Fool said, "I take my young lord to be a very melancholy man."

"What have you seen that makes you think so?" the Countess asked.

"Why, he will look at his boot and sing, he will mend the flap of his top-boot and sing, he will ask questions and sing, he will pick his teeth and sing. I know a man who had this trick of melancholy; he sold a splendid manor for a song."

"Let me see what he writes, and when he means to come," the Countess said.

She opened and read the letter that the Fool had brought to her.

The Fool said, "I have no mind to Isbel since I was at court: our old ling and our Isbels of the country are nothing like your old ling and your Isbels of the court."

"Old ling" means "salted codfish." In this society, the word "salt" is an adjective meaning "lecherous," and "cod" is a word meaning "male genitals," so the Fool was using the phrase "old ling" to refer to men. He meant that the men and the women of the French King's court were superior to the men and women of Count Rousillon's court, and so he cared no longer for the Isbel in Rousillon.

The Fool continued, "My Cupid's brains are knocked out, and I begin to love, as an old man loves money, with no stomach."

Reading the letter, the Countess said, "What have we here?"

The Fool replied, "Exactly what you are holding in your hand."

He exited.

The Countess read out loud her son's letter to her:

"I have sent you a daughter-in-law: She has healed the King, and ruined me. I have wedded her, but not bedded her; and I have sworn to make the 'not' eternal."

In fact, Bertram had sworn to make the 'not' eternal in more ways than one. He had sworn not to bed Helena eternally, and in the wedding ceremony he had sworn to make the marriage knot eternal. In addition, the maidenhead is known as the hymen or virginal knot, and in swearing not to bed her, he was swearing to let her keep her virginal knot forever.

The Countess continued to read the letter out loud:

"You shall hear I have run away. I am writing you so that you know it before the report comes. If there is room enough in the world, I will stay a long distance away from Rousillon. My duty to you. Your unfortunate son, BERTRAM."

The Countess said, "This is not done well, rash and unbridled boy. You have fled from the favors of such a good King, and you pour his indignation upon your head because you hold in contempt a virgin maiden who is too virtuous to be held in contempt by an Emperor."

The Fool came into the room and said, "Oh, madam, yonder is heavy news within; it comes from two soldiers and my young lady!"

"What is the matter?" the Countess asked.

"There is some comfort in the news, some comfort: Your son will not be killed as soon as I thought he would," the Fool said.

"Why should he be killed?" the Countess asked.

"That's what I say, madam, if he runs away, as I hear he does," the Fool said. "The danger is in standing to it; that's the loss of men, though it be the begetting of children."

The Fool was punning. A soldier standing in the line of fire can be shot and killed, so running away improves the soldier's chance of survival. "Standing" is also something that a penis does, and that can lead to the begetting of children. Both military men and fathers-to-be die. In this society, one meaning of "to die" is "to have an orgasm."

The Fool continued, "Here they come, and they will tell you more. As for my part, I heard only that your son has run away."

The Fool exited.

Helena and the two gentlemen who had recently arrived walked over to the Countess.

The first gentleman said to the Countess, "May God save you, good madam."

Helena said to her, "Madam, my lord and husband is gone, forever gone."

The second gentleman said, "Don't say that."

"Be calm," the Countess advised Helena.

The Countess then said, "Please, gentlemen, I have felt so many sudden strokes of joy and grief that the first appearance of neither, suddenly, can make me act like a woman and cry. Please tell me where my son is."

She had felt so many strokes of joy and grief that not knowing which to feel — What had happened to her son? Something good or something bad? Was he dead or alive? — made her cry from vexation.

The second gentleman replied, "Madam, he's gone to serve the Duke of Florence. We met him as he was going there, for from there we came, and, after attending to some business in hand here at the court, thither we travel again."

Helena said, "I have a letter from him to me, madam; it gives me license to travel the world as a beggar."

She read the letter out loud:

"*When you can get the ring upon my finger, a ring that shall never come off, and when you can show me a child whom I am father to and who has been born from your body, then call me your husband, but instead of such a 'then' I write a 'never.' You shall never meet these two conditions.*"

Helena said, "This is a dreadful sentence."

The Countess asked, "Did you bring this letter, gentlemen?"

The first gentleman replied, "Yes, madam, we did. But considering the contents of the letter, we are sorry that we did."

The Countess said to Helena, "Please, lady, have a better mood and disposition. If you appropriate all the griefs and say that they are yours, you rob me of a share of them. He was my son, but I wash his name out of my blood, and you are my only child."

She asked the gentlemen, "My son is headed toward Florence, is that right?"

"Yes, madam," the second gentleman said.

"And his intention is to become a soldier?"

The second gentleman said, "Such is his noble purpose; and believe it, the Duke of Florence will lay upon him all the honor that good fitness claims."

"Will you return there?" the Countess asked.

"Yes, madam," the first gentleman replied, "with the swiftest wing of speed."

Helena read out loud another line from the letter: "*Until I have no wife, I have nothing in France.*"

She said, "It is bitter."

The Countess asked, "He wrote that in his letter?"

"Yes, madam."

The first gentleman said, "It is but the boldness of his hand, perhaps, which his heart was not consenting to. He may have written something that he does not mean."

The Countess said, "Nothing in France, until he has no wife! There's nothing here that is too good for him except only his wife, and she deserves a lord whom twenty such rude boys might tend upon and call her each hour mistress."

One meaning of the word "mistress" was "female boss."

She asked the two gentlemen, "Who was with him?"

The first gentleman replied, "Only a servant, and a gentleman whom I have for some time known."

"The gentleman was Parolles, wasn't he?" the Countess asked.

"Yes, my good lady," the first gentlemen said. "It was he."

"He is a very tainted fellow, and full of wickedness," the Countess said. "Because of the bad influence of Parolles, my son corrupts the goodness he inherited."

"Indeed, good lady," the first gentleman said, "Parolles has over your son a good deal too much of bad influence, which greatly profits him."

"You're welcome, gentlemen," the Countess said. "I will entreat you, when you see my son, to tell him that his sword can never win the honor that he loses. I will write more that I will entreat you to take to him."

"We serve you, madam," the second gentleman said, "in that, and in all your worthiest affairs."

"That is not so, except as we mutually serve each other," the Countess replied. "Please come with me."

The Countess and the two gentlemen exited.

Alone, Helena said to herself, "'*Until I have no wife, I have nothing in France.*' Nothing in France, until he has no wife! You shall have no wife, Rousillon, none in France. That way, you will have everything again. Poor lord! Is it I who am chasing you from your country and exposing those tender limbs of yours to the events of the none-sparing war? And is it I who am driving you from the light-hearted, sportive court, where you were shot at with fair eyes, to a battlefield where you will be the mark of smoky muskets? Oh, you bullets, you leaden messengers, that ride upon the violent speed of fire, may you fly with false aim. May you move the always-peering air that sings with piercing."

Helena wanted all the bullets fired at her husband to miss him. If they were to pierce and pass through anything, let it be the air, which sings with a sound as the bullets pass through it. The air is a match for — a peer or equal of — the bullets. No matter how many bullets pierce and pass through the air, the air is not wounded. Bullets cannot conquer it. And the air does not wound or conquer the bullets.

Helena continued, "Bullets, do not touch my lord and husband. Whoever shoots at him, I am the person who set him there to be shot. Whoever charges on his forward — in the front lines — breast, I am the caitiff who made him be present there to be charged upon. And, although I do not kill him, I am the cause and the reason why his death was so effected. It would be better if I met the ravenous, starving lion when it roared with the sharp constraint of hunger. It would be better if all the miseries that nature owns were mine at once. No, come home, Count of Rousillon, my husband, from the dangerous place where honor wins a scar, and where as often it loses everything, including life.

"I will be gone from France. My being here keeps you there. Shall I stay here to keep you there? No, no, even if the air of Paradise fanned the house and angels did all the work of servants. I will be gone so that rumor, pitying you, may report my flight to you and console your ear. Come, night; end, day! For with the dark, I, the poor thief who stole a husband, will steal away."

— 3.3 —

The Duke of Florence, Bertram, Parolles, some soldiers, a drummer, and some trumpeters stood in front of the Duke's palace.

The Duke of Florence said to Bertram, "You are the general of our cavalry; and we, great in our hope, wager our best love and faith upon your promising fortune."

Bertram replied, "Sir, it is a charge of responsibility too heavy for my strength, but yet we'll strive to bear it for your worthy sake to the extreme edge of hazard."

"Then go you forth," the Duke of Florence said, "and may Lady Fortune play upon your prosperous helmet and be your auspicious mistress!"

Bertram prayed to Mars, god of war, "This very day, great Mars, I put myself into your file of soldiers. Make me but like my thoughts, and I shall prove to be a lover of your drum, and a hater of love."

The Countess of Rousillon and the Steward talked together in a room of the Count of Rousillon's palace. The Steward, who was named Rinaldo, had delivered to the Countess a letter that Helena had given to him the previous night.

"Alas!" the Countess said. "And would you take the letter from her? Didn't you know she would do as she has done, by sending me a letter? Read it again."

The Steward read the letter, which was written in the form of a sonnet, out loud:

"*I am Saint Jaques' pilgrim, thither gone:*

"*Ambitious love hath so in me offended,*

"*That barefoot plod I the cold ground upon,*

"*With sainted [saintly] vow my faults [sins] to have amended.*

"*Write, write, so that from the bloody course of war*

"*My dearest master, your dear son, may hie* [hurry]*:*

"*Bless him at home in peace, whilst I from far*

"*His name with zealous fervor sanctify:*

"*His taken* [undertaken] *labors bid him me forgive;*

"*I, his despiteful* [spiteful] *Juno, sent him forth*

"*From courtly friends* [friends connected with the court], *with camping* [living in tents set up in military camps] *foes to live,*

"*Where death and danger dogs the heels of worth:*

"*He is too good and fair for Death and me:*

"*Whom* [Death] *I myself embrace, to set him* [my husband] *free.*"

In the letter Helena said that she would be a religious pilgrim and visit the shrine of Saint Jaques. This is the shrine of Saint Jaques le Grand in Santiago le Compostela in northwestern Spain. France is between Spain and Italy. Rather than going west to Spain, Helena would go east to Florence, Italy, where her husband, Bertram, was.

In the letter she compared herself to the goddess Juno, wife of Jupiter, King of the gods. Juno had given to Hercules twelve labors that seemed impossible to accomplish. Helena's intention, she wrote, was to embrace Death and die, thus setting her husband free from his marriage.

The Countess said, "Ah, what sharp stings are in her mildest words! Rinaldo, you never lacked good sense as much as now when you let her leave in this way. Had I spoken with her, I could have well diverted her intentions, which by writing me this letter she has prevented."

"Pardon me, madam," the Steward said. "If I had given you this last night, she might have been overtaken, and yet she writes that pursuit would be only in vain."

"What angel shall bless this husband who is unworthy of his wife?" the Countess said. "He cannot thrive unless her prayers, which Heaven delights to hear and loves to grant, reprieve him from the wrath of greatest justice.

"Write, write, Rinaldo, to this husband who is unworthy of his wife. Let every word weigh heavy on — emphasize — her worth that he does weigh too lightly; that he weighs her too lightly is my greatest grief. Though he little feels it, set it down sharply.

"Dispatch the most convenient messenger: When it happens that he hears that she is gone, he will return; and I hope that she, hearing that he has returned, will speed her foot again, led here by pure love.

"Which of them — Bertram or Helena — is dearest to me, I am unable to discern.

"Provide a messenger.

"My heart is heavy, and my old age makes me weak. Grief would have tears, and sorrow bids me speak."

An old widow stood outside the walls of Florence along with her daughter, Diana. With them were her friend and neighbor Mariana and other citizens. The Florentine army had won a military victory and was returning to Florence, and the old widow and her companions had come to see the army.

The widow said, "Come, for if they approach the city, we shall entirely lose the sight."

They began to walk to a position that they thought the army would pass by.

Diana said, "They say the French Count of Rousillon has done very honorable service."

"It is reported that he has captured their greatest commander," the widow said, "and that with his own hand he slew the Duke of Siena's brother."

A military trumpet sounded from a different direction the widow and her companions expected. The sound was a tucket, which identified a particular individual.

The widow said, "We have lost our labor; they have gone a different way. Listen! You may know who is arriving by their trumpets."

"Come, let's return to Florence again, and satisfy ourselves with what other people tell us about the return of our army," Mariana said.

She then said, "Well, Diana, take heed of this French Count — the Count of Rousillon. The honor of a maiden is her name — the name of virgin — and no legacy is so rich as chastity."

The widow said to her daughter, Diana, "I have told my neighbor Mariana how you have been solicited by a gentleman who is the Count of Rousillon's companion."

"I know that knave — hang him!" Mariana said. "He is named Parolles, and he is a filthy officer — a pander — in those suggestions he makes to the young Count. Beware of both of them, Diana; their promises, enticements, oaths, tokens, and all these instruments of lust are not the things they seem to be. Many maidens have been seduced by them, and the misery is that their example, that so terribly shows the wreck of maidenhood, cannot for all that dissuade other maidens from being seduced. Instead, the other maidens are limed with the twigs that threaten them. They are like birds that have been captured in sticky birdlime. I hope I don't need to advise you further, but I hope your own grace and virtue will keep you where you are, even though there were no further danger known but the modesty that is so lost."

Of course, there was a further danger in a young woman losing her virginity before being married — pregnancy. Another danger was becoming what was known as "damaged goods"; if men knew that she had lost her virginity, they would refuse to marry her.

Diana replied, "You shall not need to fear me losing my virginity."

"I hope so," the widow said.

Helena, who was wearing the clothing of a religious pilgrim, walked toward them.

The widow said, "Look, here comes a pilgrim. I know she will lodge at my house; thither the pilgrims send one another. I'll question her."

The widow said to Helena, "May God save you, pilgrim! Whither are you bound?"

"To the shrine of Saint Jaques le Grand. Where do the palmers — religious pilgrims — lodge, I ask you?"

The widow replied, "At the inn bearing the sign of Saint Francis here beside the city gate."

"Is this the way?" Helena asked.

"Yes, indeed, it is," the widow said.

They heard military drums coming toward them.

The widow said, "Listen! They are coming this way."

She said to Helena, "If you will tarry, holy pilgrim, just until the troops have come by, I will conduct you where you shall be lodged. I will do this because I think I know your hostess as well as I know myself."

"Is the hostess yourself?" Helena asked. She had a quick intelligence.

"If that shall please you, pilgrim, yes," the widow said.

"I thank you, and I will wait until you have leisure to show me the way," Helena said.

"You came, I think, from France?"

"I did so."

"Here you shall see a countryman of yours who has done worthy service," the widow said.

"What is his name, please?" Helena asked.

"The Count Rousillon. Do you know such a person?"

"Only by hearsay, and what I have heard describes him as being very noble. I don't know what he looks like."

Diana said, "Whatever he is, he's well esteemed here. He stole away from France, it is reported, because the King had married him against his liking. Do you think it is true?"

"Yes, certainly, it is entirely the truth," Helena said. "I know his wife."

"A gentleman who serves the Count of Rousillon reports only coarse things about her," Diana said.

Helena asked, "What's his name?"

"Monsieur Parolles," Diana said.

"Oh, I believe the same as him," Helena said. "As the subject of praise, or compared to the worth of the great Count of Rousillon himself, she is too mean and common to have her name repeated. All her merit is a well-guarded chastity — I have not heard her chastity questioned."

"Alas, poor lady!" Diana said. "It is a hard bondage to become the wife of a husband who detests her!"

The widow said, "I am sure, good creature, that wherever she is, her heart weighs sadly. This young maiden here — my daughter, Diana — might do her a shrewd turn, if she pleased."

Displaying her quick intelligence, Helena asked, "How do you mean? Is it perhaps that the amorous Count solicits her for an unlawful purpose?"

"He does indeed," the widow said, "and he bargains with all who can in such a suit corrupt the tender honor of a maiden. But she is armed for him and keeps her guard in the most honest defense of her chastity."

Mariana said, "May the gods forbid she do anything else!"

"Now the soldiers are coming," the widow said.

Drums sounded, and flags fluttered. Bertram, Parolles, and other soldiers marched into view.

The widow pointed out some notable soldiers: "That is Antonio, the Duke of Florence's eldest son. That is Escalus."

"Which is the Frenchman?" Helena asked.

Diana pointed and said, "He is the soldier with the plume. He is a very gallant fellow. I wish that he loved his wife. If he would be more virtuous, he would be much better looking. But isn't he a handsome gentleman?"

"I like him well," Helena said.

"It is a pity he is not virtuous," Diana said. "There's that same knave who leads him to these places."

She was unwilling to use the word "brothels."

She continued, "If I were his wife, I would poison that vile rascal."

"Which is he?" Helena said.

"That jackanapes — buffoon — wearing all the military sashes," Diana said. "Why is he melancholy?"

"Perhaps he was hurt in the battle," Helena said.

Parolles said to himself, "Lose our drum! Damn!"

The military drum was a symbol of regimental honor, just like the military colors — the flag.

Mariana said, "He's shrewdly vexed at something. Look, he has spied us."

"Indeed!" the widow said, looking at Parolles. "Hang you!"

Mariana said, "And hang your courtesy, because you are a ring-carrier!"

A ring-carrier is a pander, a go-between. Parolles was currently engaged in trying to convince Diana to sleep with Bertram. The pander could carry a real ring, or the promise of a ring. Many maidens give up their virginity to men who falsely promised to marry them.

Bertram, Parolles, and the other soldiers exited.

"The troop is past," the widow said. "Come, pilgrim, I will bring you to where you shall stay. Of penitents bound by oath there's four or five already at my house who are heading to the shrine of great Saint Jaques."

"I humbly thank you," Helena said. "If it pleases this matron and this gentle maiden to eat with us tonight, I will gratefully pay the charge, and to reward you further, I will bestow some precepts on this virgin that are worthy of note."

They replied, "We accept your offer kindly."

Bertram and two French lords spoke together in their military camp near Florence. The two French lords, who were brothers named Dumain, had earlier visited the Countess of Rousillon; they had carried a letter to Helena. (See 3.2.)

The second lord said, "My good lord, put Parolles to the test; let him have his way. Let him attempt to get the regimental drum back."

The first lord said, "If your lordship does not find that he is a hilding — a good-for-nothing fellow — have no more respect for me."

"On my life, my lord, I swear that Parolles is a bubble, an empty thing," the second lord said.

"Do you think I am so far deceived in him?" Bertram said. "Do you really think that I am that mistaken in my estimate of his character?"

"Believe it, my lord," the second lord said. "To my own direct knowledge, without any malice, and speaking about him as if he were my relative, he's a most notable coward, an infinite and endless liar, an hourly promise-breaker, the owner of not one good quality worthy your lordship's maintenance. You pay for his food and lodging, but trust me, he is not worth the expense."

"It is fitting that you know him for what he is," the first lord said, "lest, with you trusting too much in his virtue, which he doesn't have, he might during some great and trusty business fail you in a major crisis."

"I wish I knew in what particular action I could test him," Bertram said.

"There is none better than to let him rescue his drum," the first lord said, "which you hear him say so confidently he will undertake to do."

The second lord said, "I, with a troop of Florentines, will suddenly surprise and capture him; such soldiers I will have, whom I am sure he will think are from the enemy. We will bind and hoodwink — blindfold — him so that he shall suppose no other but that he is carried into the military camp of the adversaries, when in reality we will bring him to our own tents. Your lordship should be present at his examination. If, for the promise of sparing his life and in the highest compulsion of base fear, he does not offer to betray you and deliver all the intelligence in his power against you, and that with the divine forfeit of his soul upon oath, never trust my judgment in anything. He will betray you in return for the promise that his life will be spared."

"Oh, for the love of laughter," the first lord said, "let him 'rescue' his drum from the enemy. He says he has a stratagem to do it. When your lordship sees the bottom — the complete lack — of his success in it, and to what metal, as well as mettle, this counterfeit lump of ore will be melted, if you do not give him John Drum's entertainment, your inclination to like him cannot be removed."

"John Drum's entertainment" means "rejection" and "unceremonious dismissal."

The first lord then looked up and said, "Here he comes."

Parolles walked over to the group.

The second lord whispered to Bertram, "Oh, for the love of laughter, do not hinder the honor of his design. Let him rescue and fetch away from the enemy his drum in any case."

"How are you now, monsieur!" Bertram said to Parolles. "This drum sticks sorely in your disposition — it wounds your state of mind."

"A plague on it!" the first lord said. "Let it go! It is only a drum."

"'Only a drum'!" Parolles said. "Is it 'only a drum'? A drum lost in that way! That was an 'excellent' command — to charge in with our cavalry upon our own flanks, and to attack our own soldiers!"

The first lord said, "That was not to be blamed upon the command of the military engagement. It was a disaster of war that Julius Caesar himself could not have prevented, if he had been there to command."

"Well, we cannot greatly condemn our success," Bertram said. "We won the battle, but we suffered some dishonor in the loss of that drum, and that drum cannot be recovered."

"It might have been recovered," Parolles said.

"It might," Bertram said, "but it cannot now be recovered."

"It is to be recovered," Parolles said. "Except that the merit of service is seldom attributed to the true and exact performer — all too often people don't receive the credit they deserve for their accomplishments; that credit goes to people who don't deserve it — I would have that drum or another like it, or '*hic jacet*.'"

"*Hic jacet*" is Latin for "Here lies." It was the beginning of many epitaphs. Parolles was saying that if he could be sure to get the credit he would deserve, he would get the drum back or die in the attempt.

Bertram said, "Why, if you have a stomach — the courage — for it, monsieur, if you think your practical skills in strategy can bring this instrument of honor again into its native quarter, then be courageous and of great spirit in the enterprise and go on and do it. I will honor the attempt for a worthy exploit: if you speed well and succeed in it, the Duke shall both speak of it and extend to you what further becomes his greatness, even to the utmost syllable of your worthiness. The Duke shall reward you well with words and with material gifts."

"By the hand of a soldier, I swear that I will undertake it," Parolles said.

"But you must not now slumber in it," Bertram said. "You must act quickly."

"I'll go about it this evening," Parolles said, "and I will immediately write down the problems I will need to solve, encourage myself in my certainty of overcoming those problems, and put myself into my mortal preparation for either suffering death or causing others to suffer it. By midnight look to hear further from me."

"May I be bold enough to acquaint his grace the Duke of Florence that you are going to get the drum back?" Bertram asked.

"I don't know what the outcome of my attempt will be, my lord," Parolles said, "but I vow to attempt to recover the drum."

"I know you are valiant," Bertram said, "and I will vouch for the capability of your soldiership. Farewell."

"I do not love many words," Parolles said, and then he exited.

The second lord said, "He does not love many words — no more than a fish loves water. Isn't this a strange fellow, my lord, who so confidently seems to undertake this business, which he knows is not to be done? He says that he will be damned if he doesn't do this act, and yet he would rather be damned than to do it."

The first lord said to Bertram, "You do not know him, my lord, as we do. It is certain that he will steal himself into a man's favor and for a week escape a great deal of discoveries, but when you find him out, you have him ever after. Parolles can fool a man for a week, but then the man wises up and knows Parolles' true character forever."

Bertram said, "Do you think he will make no attempt at all of doing this thing that he so seriously says that he will do?"

"He will make no attempt, none in the world," the second lord said. "Instead, he will return with an invented story and clap upon you two or three probable lies, but we have almost hunted him down. You shall see his fall tonight; for indeed he is not worthy of your lordship's respect."

"We'll make some entertainment for you with the fox before we metaphorically skin him," the first lord said. "He was first smoked out and exposed by the old lord Lafeu. When Parolles' disguise and he are parted, tell me what a sprat — a small fish — you shall find him. You shall see that he is a sprat this very night."

"I must go look after my twigs," the second lord said. "He shall be caught."

The twigs were metaphorical and referred to a trap. Twigs and branches were coated with sticky birdlime as a way to catch birds.

"Your brother shall go along with me," Bertram said to the second lord.

"As it pleases your lordship," the second lord said. "I'll leave you."

He exited.

Bertram said to the first lord, "Now I will lead you to the house, and show you the lass I spoke of."

"But you say she's chaste," the first lord said.

"That's her only fault," Bertram said. "I spoke with her only once and found her wondrously cold, but I sent to her, by this same foolish coxcomb — Parolles — whom we have in the wind, tokens and letters that she sent back to me, and this is all I have done. She's a beautiful creature. Will you go with me and see her?"

"With all my heart, my lord."

Helena and the widow spoke together in a room in the widow's house.

Helena said, "If you doubt that I am Bertram's wife, I don't know how I shall assure you further without losing the grounds I work upon. In order for my plan to work, I need to keep my presence in Florence hidden from my husband."

"Although my estate has fallen, I was well born," the widow said. "I have never been acquainted with this kind of business, and I would not expose my reputation now to any act that might stain it."

"Nor would I wish you to," Helena said. "First, trust me when I say that the Count of Rousillon is my husband. Also trust that what I have spoken to you with your sworn secrecy is true from word to word. If you do these two things, then you cannot err by bestowing the good aid that I shall borrow from you."

"I should believe you," the widow said, "for you have showed me that which well proves you're great in fortune."

"Take this purse of gold," Helena said, "and let me buy thus far your friendly help, which I will overpay and pay again when I have found it. The Count woos your daughter, lays down his wanton siege before her beauty, and is resolved to seduce her. Let her finally say that she consents; we will direct her in the best way to do it.

"Right now his importunate blood will deny her nothing that she'll demand. The Count wears a ring that has passed downward in his house from son to son, some four or five generations since the first father wore it. This ring he values very richly, yet in his mad fire, to buy the means by which to satisfy his lust, this ring would not seem too dear to him to give up, however much he repents giving it up after he satisfies his lust."

"Now I see what you intend to do with your plan," the widow said.

"You see that it is lawful, then," Helena said. "It is no more than that your daughter, before she pretends to be won, desires this ring to be given to her. She will set up a place and a time where and when she is supposed to sleep with him. But she will allow me to sleep with him while she herself is most chastely absent. After this is done, to her dowry I'll add three thousand crowns to what has passed to you already."

"I have yielded," the widow said. "I will do it. Give my daughter instructions for how she shall proceed so that the time and place for this very lawful deceit may prove fitting and agreeable. Every night he comes with musicians of all sorts and songs composed to seduce her. From our eaves we command him to go away, but he persists as if his life depends on it."

"Why then tonight let us put our plot in motion," Helena said. "If it succeeds, it is a wicked meaning in a lawful deed and a lawful meaning in a lawful act, where both do not sin, and yet it is a sinful fact."

If Helena slept with her husband, they would not be doing a sinful act because they were married. However, Helena had to do a sinful act — deceive her husband — in order to get her husband to sleep with her. In addition, her husband, although he was not in fact committing adultery, thought that he was sleeping with a woman who was not his wife. Despite the deceit committed, or thought to be committed, they were still doing a lawful act.

Helena then said to the widow, "But let's go about setting this plot in motion."

CHAPTER 4
— 4.1 —

Outside the Florentine military camp, the second French lord and five or six soldiers waited to ambush Parolles.

The second French lord said, "He can come no other way but by this hedge-corner. When you burst out of hiding upon him, speak whatever terrible language you will. Although you don't understand it yourselves, it doesn't matter, for we must not seem to understand him unless we have someone among us whom we produce to be an interpreter."

The first soldier said, "Good Captain, let me be the interpreter."

"Aren't you acquainted with him?" the second lord asked. "Does he know your voice?"

"No, sir, I promise you," the first soldier replied.

The second lord asked, "But what linsey-woolsey will you reply to us?"

Literally, linsey-woolsey is cloth made of linen and wool. Figuratively, it is a mishmash of language.

"Even such as you speak to me," the first soldier replied.

The second lord said, "Parolles must think that we are some band of foreign soldiers in the enemy's payroll. Be aware that he has a smack of all neighboring languages; therefore, we must everyone be a man of his own fancy and not know what we speak one to another — as long as we seem to know what we speak to each other, we will know enough for our purpose. The language of jackdaws is gabble enough and good enough. As for you, interpreter, you must seem very intelligent. But crouch and lie in ambush! Here he comes, to pass two hours in a nap, and then to return and swear to the lies he invents."

Parolles walked onto the scene, unaware that soldiers were crouching in ambush.

"Ten o'clock," he said. "After no longer than three hours, it will be time enough to go home. What shall I say I have done? It must be a very plausible lie that carries it off. They begin to smoke me out and expose me, and disgraces have recently knocked too often at my door. I find that my tongue is too foolhardy, but my heart has the fear of Mars and of his creatures before it, not daring to do the reports of my tongue. I don't dare do what my tongue says I will do."

The second lord said quietly so that Parolles could not hear him, "This is the first truth that your own tongue was ever guilty of."

"What the devil should move me to undertake the recovery of this drum, being not ignorant of the impossibility, and knowing I had no such intention?" Parolles said. "I must give myself some wounds, and say I got them in the exploit of recovering the drum, yet slight wounds will not carry it off. They will say, 'Did you come away with such slight wounds?' And great wounds I dare not give myself. Wherefore, what's the physical evidence I can show them? Tongue, I must put you into a dairy woman's mouth and buy myself another tongue from Bajazet's mule, if you prattle me into these perils."

Dairy women were known for being talkative.

Bajazet was a character in a Turkish history who rode a mule. Why would Parolles want to buy a tongue from a Turkish mule? It would be better for him to have a tongue that cannot speak any human language than to have a tongue that continually got him into trouble. When it comes to human language, mules are mutes, and Turkish mutes are slaves who are forced to remain mute because their tongues have been cut out. It would be better for Parolles to have no tongue — or a tongue that has been cut out — than to have a tongue that continually got him into trouble.

The second lord said, "Is it possible he should know what he is, and still be what he is? Wouldn't he try to change and become better?"

Parolles said, "I wish the cutting of my garments would serve the turn, or the breaking of my Spanish sword. I need to produce some evidence intended to show that I have been fighting."

"We won't let you off so easily," the second lord said.

Parolles said, "Or I could shave my beard, and then say I did it as part of a stratagem."

"It would not work," the second lord said.

"Or I could drown my clothes in a stream or river, and say I was stripped," Parolles said.

"That would hardly serve," the second lord said.

"Suppose I swore I leaped from the window of the citadel," Parolles said.

"How high would the window be?" the second lord said to himself.

"Thirty fathoms," Parolles said, thinking out loud to himself. "One hundred and eighty feet."

"Three great oaths would scarcely make that be believed," the second lord said.

"I wish I had any drum of the enemy's," Parolles said. "I would swear I recovered it."

"You shall hear one soon," the second lord said.

"A drum now of the enemy's —" Parolles mused.

A drum sounded, and the soldiers ambushed Parolles.

The second lord began to speak nonsense: "*Throca movousus, cargo, cargo, cargo.*"

The other soldiers replied with more nonsense: "*Cargo, cargo, cargo, villiando par corbo, cargo.*"

"*Cargo*" is Spanish for "charge."

The soldiers seized him.

"Oh, ransom me, ransom me!" Parolles cried.

He wanted to be held for ransom rather than killed.

The soldiers blindfolded him, and he cried, "Do not cover my eyes."

The first soldier said, "*Boskos thromuldo boskos.*"

Parolles said, "I know you are the Muscovites' regiment, and I shall lose my life for lack of knowing your language. If there be anyone here who is German, or Dane, low Dutch, Italian, or French, let him speak to me. I'll reveal information that shall lead to the defeat and ruin of the Duke of Florence."

"*Boskos vauvado,*" the first soldier said. "I understand you, and I can speak your tongue. *Kerely bonto,* sir, betake yourself to your faith and say your prayers, for seventeen daggers are at your bosom."

"Oh!" Parolles cried.

"Oh, pray, pray, pray!" the first soldier said. "*Manka revania dulche.*"

"*Revania*" is Hungarian for "screeching," and "*dulce*" is Latin for "sweet."

The second lord said loudly, "*Oscorbidulchos volivorco.*"

"The general is content to spare you yet," the first soldier said. "And, blindfolded as you are, he will lead you on to gather information from you. Perhaps you may give him information that will save your life."

"Oh, let me live!" Parolles cried. "And all the secrets of our military camp I'll reveal: the strength of their force and their plans. I'll speak wonders."

"But will you do so truly and faithfully?" the first soldier asked.

"If I do not, damn me," Parolles said.

"*Acordo linta*," the first soldier said. "Come on; you are granted a space of time to live."

"*Linta*" is Portugese for "agreement."

Some soldiers took Parolles away.

The second lord said, "Go, tell the Count Rousillon and my brother that we have caught the woodcock, and we will keep him muffled and quiet until we hear from them."

A woodcock is an easily captured bird that was thought to be stupid.

The second soldier replied, "Captain, I will."

The second lord said, "Parolles will betray us all unto ourselves. He will tell us everything although he thinks that we are the enemy. Inform the Count Rousillon and my brother about that."

"I will do so, sir," the second soldier replied.

"Until then I'll keep him in the dark and safely locked up," the second lord said.

Bertram and Diana talked together in the widow's house.

Bertram said, "They told me that your name was Fontibell."

"No, my good lord, my name is Diana."

Bertram wasn't much of a lover: He couldn't even remember her name. Of course, he had heard that her name was Diana, but in trying to remember it, the image of a fountain with a statue of Diana came to mind, and he mistakenly thought that her name was "Fontibell," a name that means "Beautiful Fountain."

"You are named after a goddess," Bertram said, "and you are worthy of your name, with additional titles! But, fair soul, in your fine frame does love have no position? If the quick fire of youth does not light up your mind, you are no maiden, but a monument — a tomb. When you are dead, you will be such a one as you are now, for you are cold and stern, and now you should be as your mother was when your sweet self was begotten."

"When I was begotten, my mother was chaste and did not engage in illicit sex," Diana said. "She was married."

"So should you be," Bertram said.

False promises of marriage are part of the arsenal of the seducer.

"No," Diana said. "My mother did but such duty as, my lord, you owe to your wife."

"Speak no more of that," Bertram said. "I ask you, do not strive against my vows. Do not resist me because of my marriage vows. I was compelled to marry her, but I love you by love's own sweet constraint, and I will forever do you all rights of service."

"Yes, you men serve us women until we sexually serve you," Diana said, "but when you have our roses — our maidenheads — you barely leave our thorns to prick ourselves with regret and you mock our bareness."

"How I have sworn that I will serve you!" Bertram said.

"It is not the many oaths that make the truth," Diana said, "but the plain single vow that is vowed truly. The number of oaths is not important; what is important is whether the oath is sworn morally and with sincerity. What is not holy, that we swear not by, but instead we take the Highest to witness our oath.

So then, please, tell me, if I should swear by God's great attributes that I loved you dearly, would you believe my oaths when I did love you ill — when my love for you is ill?"

Bertram's "love" for Diana was ill; he wanted to seduce her and then abandon her.

Diana continued, "To swear by him whom I profess to love, and yet to work against him and make him sin by committing adultery has no logic. Therefore, your oaths are mere words and a poor contract that lacks the seal that would make it legally binding, at least in my opinion."

"Change it! Change your opinion!" Bertram urged. "Be not so holy-cruel — so cruel by being holy! Love is holy, and my integrity never knew the crafty plots that you charge men with engaging in. Stand off no more, but give yourself to my lovesick desires, which then will recover. Say that you are mine, and my love as it begins shall ever so persevere."

Diana said, "I see that men make ropes in such a scarre so that we'll forsake ourselves."

This may sound like nonsense, but that is because she was using obsolete words. According to the *Oxford English Dictionary*, a rope is "[o]utcry, clamour; cries of distress or lamentation." Also according to the *Oxford English Dictionary*, "scarre" can be a spelling of "scare," which can mean "[f]ear, dread." By the way, the Norwegian verb "*rope*" means "shout, scream, call."

Therefore, this is what Diana was saying: "I see that men make cries of distress when they are afraid they won't get what they want so that we women will forsake ourselves." In other words, men will say anything to get immoral sex.

She then pointed to a ring on Bertram's hand and said, "Give me that ring."

"I'll lend it to you, my dear," Bertram said, "but I have no power to give it to you."

"Won't you give it to me, my lord?" Diana asked.

"It is an honor — an heirloom — belonging to our house, bequeathed down from many ancestors," Bertram said. "It would be the greatest disgrace in the world for me to lose its possession."

"My honor's such a ring as that," Diana said. "My chastity's the jewel of our house, bequeathed down from many ancestors; it would be the greatest disgrace in the world for me to lose my chastity. Thus your own proper wisdom brings in the champion Honor on my side, against your vain assault on my chastity."

"Here, take my ring," Bertram said, giving her the ring. "May my house, my honor, and indeed, my life be yours, and I'll be commanded by you."

"When midnight comes, knock at my bedchamber-window," Diana said. "I'll arrange things so that my mother shall not hear. Now I will charge you in the bond of truth, when you have conquered my yet maiden bed, to remain there only an hour and do not speak to me. My reasons are very strong; and you shall know them when this ring shall be delivered back to you again. And on your finger in the night I'll put another ring, so that what in time proceeds may betoken to the future our past deeds."

In the marriage ceremony, the man and the woman exchange rings. Helena, of course, would be the woman in bed with Bertram, who could remain only an hour with her and not talk to her because Helena did not want to be recognized by the sound of her voice or to be seen in the morning light. She did, however, want to spend some time with Bertram after sex.

Diana said, "Adieu, until then; then, don't fail to appear. You have won a wife of me, although there my hope is done. Once I give up my virginity in this manner, I also give up my hope of ever becoming a wife."

In fact, Bertram would win a wife — Helena — from Diana.

Bertram said, "A heaven on earth I have won by wooing you."

He exited.

Diana said, "For which live long to thank both Heaven and me!"

Their ideas of heaven/Heaven were different.

Diana continued, "You may do so in the end. My mother told me just how he would woo, as if she sat in his heart; she says all men have the same oaths. He has sworn to marry me when his wife's dead; therefore, I'll lie with him when I am buried. Since Frenchmen weave plots as if they were weaving a braid, let those marry who will — I intend to live and die a maiden. But I think it no sin to deceive and cozen and cheat him who would unjustly win."

The two French lords spoke together in the Florentine camp. Some soldiers were present.

The first lord said, "You have not given Bertram his mother's letter?"

"I delivered it an hour ago," the second lord said. "There is something in it that stings his nature, for as he read it he changed almost into another man."

"He is very much worthy of the blame laid upon him for shaking off so good a wife and so sweet a lady," the first lord said. "He rejected his wife, who is a good woman."

"He especially has incurred the everlasting displeasure of the King, who had even tuned his bounty to sing happiness to him," the second lord said. "The King would have made him a very wealthy and much-respected man. I will tell you something about Bertram, but you must let it dwell darkly with you. Don't tell anyone."

"When you have spoken it, it is dead, and I am its grave," the first lord said.

"Bertram has perverted a young gentlewoman here in Florence, of a most chaste reputation, and this night he fleshes his sexual desire in the spoil of her honor," the second lord said. "He has given her his ancestral ring, which is an heirloom, and he thinks himself a made man in the unchaste arrangement."

The second lord was using a hunting term when he used the word "fleshes." When a dog makes a kill while hunting, it is rewarded with a piece of the flesh of the kill.

"Now, may God delay our rebellion!" the first lord said. "All of us sin and rebel against God, but let us fight temptation and put off sinning as long as possible. As we are ourselves — that is, without the benefit of the grace of God — what things are we!"

"We are entirely our own traitors," the second lord said. "We are traitors to the person whom we ought to be. And as in the common course of all treasons, we always see the traitors reveal themselves with boasting conversation until they attain their abhorred aims, with the result that he who in this action plots against his own nobility in his proper stream overflows and destroys himself. That is, he who plots against his own nobility will succeed and will undo his own nobility with his own plots. His nobility ought to stay in its own proper course, but by giving in to his evil impulses the man destroys himself as if he has been caught in an overflowing flood."

The first lord said, "Isn't it a sign of damnation in us to be trumpeters of our unlawful intents? Bertram has been boasting about corrupting a chaste and virtuous maiden. Shall we not then have his company tonight?"

"Not until after midnight," the second lord said, "for his schedule is full until that hour."

"Midnight approaches quickly," the first lord said. "I would gladly have him see his companion — Parolles — dissected, so that he might take a measure of his own judgments, wherein so curiously he had set this counterfeit. Bertram is wrong in his opinion of Parolles; if he can realize that, he may realize that he is wrong in his opinion of his wife. Up until now, Bertram has treated Parolles as if he were a precious jewel, but we know that Parolles is a counterfeit gem that has until now been put in an elaborate setting."

"We will not meddle with Parolles until Bertram comes," the second lord said, "for the presence of the one must be the whip of the other."

Both Parolles and Bertram will be the whip of the other. Parolles will be exposed as a coward in the presence of Bertram, but Bertram will realize his mistaken judgment of Parolles in the presence of Parolles.

"In the meantime, what do you hear about these wars?" the first lord asked.

"I hear there is an overture of peace," the second lord said.

"I assure you, a peace has been reached," the first lord said.

"What will Count Rousillon do then?" the second lord asked. "Will he travel further, or will he return again to France?"

"I perceive, by this question," the first lord said, "that you are not altogether of his council. You do not give him counsel."

"Let it be forbid, sir," the second lord said. "If that were true, I would be a great deal responsible for his act — this seduction, which, we know, is unethical."

"Sir, his wife some two months ago fled from his house," the first lord said. "Her intention was a pilgrimage to Saint Jaques le Grand, which holy undertaking with most austere sanctity she accomplished, and while she resided there the tenderness of her nature became as a prey to her grief. In the end, she made a groan with her last breath, and now she sings in Heaven. She died."

"How is this known to be true?" the second lord asked.

"The stronger, more convincing evidence of its truth is by her own letters, which shows her story to be true, even to the point of her death," the first lord said. "Her death itself, which she herself could not say had come, was faithfully and truly confirmed by the rector of the place."

"Does Count Rousillon have all this information?" the second lord asked.

"Yes," the first lord said, "and he has the particular confirmations, point from point and in every detail confirmed, to the full substantiation of the truth."

"I am heartily sorry that he'll be glad of this," the second lord said.

"How mightily sometimes we make for ourselves comforts of our losses!" the first lord said.

"And how mightily some other times we drown our gain in tears!" the second lord said. "The great dignity and respect that his valor has here acquired for him shall at home be encountered with a shame as ample."

"The web of our life is of a mingled yarn, good and ill together," the first lord said. "Our virtues would cause us to be proud, if our sins did not whip us, and our sins would cause us to despair, if we did not cherish our virtues."

A servant entered the room.

The first lord asked, "Where's Bertram, your master?"

"He met the Duke of Florence in the street, sir, from whom he has taken a solemn leave," the servant replied. "His lordship will leave tomorrow morning for France. The Duke of Florence has offered him letters praising him to the King of France."

"They shall be no more than is needful there, even if they were more than they can commend," the second lord said.

"They cannot be too sweet for the King's tartness," the second lord said.

The King of France was angry at Bertram because of Bertram's poor treatment of Helena, and so Bertram needed the very highest commendations he could get.

He looked up and said, "Here's his lordship now."

Bertram entered the room.

"How are you now, my lord!" the second lord said. "Isn't it after midnight?"

"I have this night dispatched sixteen pieces of business, which could each have taken a month to sort out. Here's a list of the pieces of business that I have undertaken with success in succession: I have taken ceremonious leave of the Duke of Florence, said my adieus to those nearest him, buried a wife, mourned for her, wrote to my mother that I am returning to France, hired my means of transportation home, and between these main parcels of dispatch effected many nicer and more trivial pieces of business; the last was the greatest, but that I have not ended yet."

The last piece of business was sleeping with "Diana," as he supposed, but that was not finished because she could become pregnant, and/or she could insist that she become his wife, as he had promised her he would when his first wife had died.

The second lord said, "If the business be of any difficulty, and in the morning you will depart from hence, it requires haste from your lordship."

"I mean, the business has not ended because I am afraid that I will hear of it hereafter," Bertram said. "But shall we have this dialogue between the fool and the soldier? Come, bring forth this counterfeit, false image of a soldier; he has deceived me, like a double-meaning, equivocating prophesier."

Some prophets use equivocation in their answers to questions. Croesus, King of Lydia, wanted to attack Persia, but first he went to the Oracle of Delphi and asked the Oracle what would happen if he attacked the mighty Kingdom of Persia. The Oracle replied, "A mighty Kingdom will fall." Lydia attacked Persia, and a mighty Kingdom did fall: the mighty Kingdom of Lydia.

"Bring Parolles forth," the second lord said. "He has sat in the stocks all night, poor gallant knave."

A person sitting in the stocks has his legs (and/or arms and/or head) restrained. The word "gallant" in this context meant "fancily dressed."

Bertram said, "It does not matter. His heels have deserved it because they have usurped his spurs for so long."

Parolles' heels ran away from battle, usurping his spurs, which ought to be used to spur his horse to go into battle. "Usurping his spurs" also meant that Parolles had falsely claimed to have knightly valor.

Bertram then asked, "How does Parolles carry himself?"

By "carry himself," Bertram meant "comport himself," aka "conduct himself."

"I have told your lordship already, the stocks carry him," the second lord said. "They carry his weight. But to answer you as you would be understood, he weeps like a wench who has spilled her milk. He has confessed his sins to Morgan, whom he supposes to be a friar, from the time he first remembers anything from his life to this very immediate disaster of his being set in the stocks, and what do you think he has confessed?"

"He has confessed nothing about me, has he?" Bertram asked.

"His confession is taken and written down, and it shall be read to his face," the second lord said. "If your lordship is in it, as I believe you are, you must be patient until you can hear it."

Parolles, blindfolded and guarded by the first soldier, walked to a place close to them.

"A plague upon him!" Bertram said. "Blindfolded! He can say nothing about me."

"Hush! Hush!" the first lord said. "Hoodman comes!"

They spoke quietly enough that Parolles could not hear them.

Hoodman was the blindfolded player in the game hoodman blind, aka blindman's buff or blindman's bluff. The word "buff" at one time meant "small push."

The first lord then began speaking nonsense: "*Portotartarosa.*"

The nonsense word included the word "Tartar"; in this society, Tartars were known for being savage. "*Porto*" is Latin for "I carry."

The first soldier said to Parolles, "He calls for the tortures. What will you tell us without your being tortured?"

"I will confess everything I know without constraint," Parolles said. "If you pinch me like a pasty, I can say no more."

A pasty is a small pastry with its crust pinched together so that the filling, often meat and vegetables, is inside. One meaning of "pinch" is "inflict bodily pain."

"*Bosko chimurcho,*" the first soldier said.

"*Bosko*" is Polish for "divinely."

"*Boblibindo chicurmurco,*" the first lord said.

"You are a merciful general," the first soldier said. "Our general orders you to answer what I shall ask you out of a list of questions."

"And I will answer with the truth, as I hope to live," Parolles said.

The first soldier read out loud, "*First demand of him how many horsemen the Duke of Florence has.*"

He asked Parolles, "What do you say to that?"

Parolles answered, "Five or six thousand, but they are very weak and unserviceable. The troops are all scattered, and the commanders are very poor rogues, I swear upon my reputation and credit and as I hope to live."

"Shall I set down your answer so?" the first soldier asked.

"Do," Parolles said. "I'll take the sacrament on it, how and in which way you will."

Some people disagreed on how to take the sacrament, whether while sitting or while kneeling.

"All's one to him — he doesn't care," Bertram said. "What a past-saving — damned to Hell — slave this man is!"

"You're deceived, my lord," the first lord said ironically. "This is Monsieur Parolles, the expert in military affairs, aka gallant militarist — that was his own phrase — who had the whole theory of war in the knot of his sash, and the practice in the chape — the metal plate where the dagger-point goes — of the sheath of his dagger. He understands both the theory and the practice of war."

A lady who favored him would knot his sash, and the chape would be of use when the dagger is not in use.

The second lord said, "I will never trust a man again because he keeps his sword clean and polished, nor will I believe he can have everything in him because he wears his apparel neatly and elegantly."

"Well, that's set down," the first soldier said.

"Five or six thousand horsemen, I said — I will say the truth — or thereabouts," Parolles said. "Set it down, for I'll speak the truth."

"He's very near the truth in this," the first lord said.

"But I will not learn words to give him thanks for it, considering the reason he delivers the truth," Bertram said.

"They are poor rogues," Parolles said. "Please, set that down in writing."

"Well, that's set down," the first soldier said.

"I humbly thank you, sir," Parolles said. "The truth's a truth: The rogues are marvelously poor."

The first soldier read out loud, "*Demand of him, of what strength they are in foot soldiers.*"

He then asked Parolles, "What do you say to that?"

Parolles replied, "Truly, sir, if I were to live only until this present hour, I will tell the truth. Let me see. Spurio has a hundred and fifty foot soldiers. Sebastian has the same number. Corambus has the same number. Jaques has the same number. Guiltian, Cosmo, Lodowick, and Gratii have two hundred and fifty foot soldiers each. My own company, as well as the companies of Chitopher, Vaumond, and Bentii have two hundred and fifty each. So the official list of men, both the rotten men and the sound men, upon my life, amounts not to fifteen thousand heads, half of whom dare not shake snow from off their military cloaks, lest they shake themselves to pieces."

Bertram asked, "What shall be done to Parolles?"

"Nothing, but let him have thanks," the first lord replied.

Presumably, Parolles would not welcome the kind of "thanks" he would receive.

The first lord added, "Ask him about my character, and what credit I have with the Duke of Florence."

The first soldier said to Parolles, "Well, that's set down."

He then read out loud, "*You shall ask him whether one Captain Dumain, a Frenchman, is in the camp; what is his reputation with the Duke; what is his valor, honesty, and expertness in wars; and you shall ask him whether he thinks it were not possible, with well-weighing sums of gold, to corrupt Captain Dumain to revolt.*"

"Well-weighing sums of gold" are "heavy amounts of gold" and "influential amounts of gold."

The first soldier asked Parolles, "What do you say about this? What do you know about it?"

"I beg you," Parolles said, "to let me answer each particular question. Ask me each question one at a time."

"Do you know this Captain Dumain?" the first soldier asked.

"I know him," Parolles said. "He was a patcher's apprentice in Paris, from whence he was whipped for getting the sheriff's fool pregnant — she was a dumb innocent who could not tell him no."

A patcher is either a cobbler who mends shoes or a tailor who mends clothing.

The sheriff would have custody of feebleminded citizens whose estates were worth little. The King would have custody of feebleminded citizens whose estates were worth much.

Captain Dumain was angry and made a motion as if he were going to attack Parolles.

Bertram said to the first lord, who was Captain Dumain, "Please, don't do anything. Restrain your anger and keep your hands away from Parolles, although I know his brains are forfeit to the next tile that falls. He is sure to meet with an 'accident' that will take his life."

The first soldier asked, "Well, is this Captain in the Duke of Florence's camp?"

"Upon my knowledge, he is, and he is lousy," Parolles said.

The word "lousy" was both an insult and literally meant. Military camps were full of lice.

Bertram looked at the first lord and stifled a laugh.

The first lord said to Bertram, "Don't look that way at me; we shall hear about your lordship soon."

The first soldier asked, "What is Captain Dumain's reputation with the Duke of Florence?"

"The Duke knows him for no other than a poor officer of mine," Parolles said, "and he wrote to me this other day to kick him out of the band of soldiers. I think I have his letter in my pocket."

"By mother Mary, we'll search your pocket for it," the first soldier said.

"In all seriousness, I do not know that it is in my pocket," Parolles said. "Either it is there, or it is in a file with the Duke's other letters in my tent."

"Here it is," the first soldier said. "Here's a paper. Shall I read it to you?"

"I don't know whether it is the Duke's letter or not," Parolles said.

"Our interpreter does his job well," Bertram said.

"Excellently," the first lord agreed.

The first soldier read out loud, "*Diana, the Count's a fool, and wealthy with gold —.*"

Parolles interrupted, "That is not the Duke's letter, sir; that is a warning to a proper maid in Florence, one named Diana, to take heed of the allurement of Bertram, Count Rousillon, a foolish idle boy, but for all that very ruttish — he is very horny. Please, sir, put away the letter."

"No, I'll read it first," the first soldier said, "if you don't mind."

"My intention in writing the letter, I say, was very honest in behalf of the maid," Parolles said, "for I knew the young Count to be a dangerous and lascivious boy, who is a whale to virginity and devours up all the fry it finds."

When it came to virgins, Bertram, according to Parolles, was like a whale feeding on large numbers of small fish.

Bertram said, "Damnable both-sides rogue! He pretends to be a friend, but he is not a friend."

The first soldier read the letter out loud:

"When he swears oaths, bid him drop gold, and take it;

"After he scores, he never pays the score.

"Half won is match well made; match, and well make it.

"He never pays after-debts, take it before.

"And say that a soldier, Diana, told you this:

"Men are to mell with, boys are not to kiss.

"You can count on this, the Count's a fool, I know it,

"Who pays before, but not when he does owe it.

"I am yours, as he vowed to you in your ear,

"PAROLLES."

His advice to Diana was to receive payment in advance for what Bertram would take away from her. Indeed, according to Parolles, the only way to get money from Bertram, who was happy to get things on credit and then never pay, was to make him pay in advance. In other words, Parolles was advising Diana, more or less, to sell her virginity. Why less? Because he — Parolles — would like her to give away her virginity to him, something he hinted at when he wrote that men are to mell — have sex — with, while boys are not worth kissing. The implication was that Bertram was a boy, while Parolles was a man. But overall, Parolles regarded sex as a woman's sellable commodity.

"Half won is match well made; match, and well make it" referred to a sexual match between Bertram and Diana. Parolles was saying this: When a match is well made, with all conditions agreed to, it is a match that is half won; therefore, continue to make the match and to make it good. In other words, Parolles wanted Diana to sell her virginity, but to get a good price for it.

Bertram said, "Parolles shall be whipped through the army with this rhyming poem written on his forehead."

The second lord said ironically, "This is your devoted friend, sir, the multiple linguist and the armipotent — mighty in arms — soldier."

"I could endure anything before but a cat, and now he's a cat to me," Bertram said.

The first soldier said, "I perceive, sir, by the General's looks, we shall be obliged to hang you."

"Give me my life, sir, in any case," Parolles pleaded. "It is not that I am afraid to die, but that, because my sins are so many, I would like to spend the remainder of my natural life in repentance. Let me live, sir, in a dungeon, in the stocks, or anywhere, as long as I may live."

"We'll see what may be done," the first soldier said, "as long as you confess freely; therefore, once more let's talk about this Captain Dumain. You have answered the question about his reputation with the Duke and about his valor. Now answer this question: How honest is he?"

"He will steal, sir, an egg out of a cloister," Parolles replied. "As for rapes and ravishments, he parallels Nessus, the Centaur who attempted to rape the wife of Hercules. He does not believe in keeping his oaths; when it comes to breaking them, he is stronger than Hercules. He will lie, sir, with such volubility and fluency that you would think truth were a fool. Drunkenness is his best virtue, for he will be swine-drunk; and in his sleep he does little harm, save to his bedclothes; but his servants know his habit of peeing the bed and so they lay him in straw. I have but little more to say, sir, about his honesty. He has everything that an honest man should not have; of what an honest man should have, he has nothing."

Impressed by Parolles' over-the-top villainy, the first lord said, "I begin to love him for this."

"For this description of your honesty?" Bertram said. "I say a pox upon him! To me, he's more and more a cat."

The first soldier asked Parolles, "What do you have to say about his expertness in war?"

"Truly, sir," Parolles said. "He has led the drum before the English tragedians."

English acting troupes used to advertise an upcoming play by parading behind a drum. Parolles was saying that Captain Dumain's experience with drums was not with military drums, but with actors' drums.

Parolles continued, "To tell lies about him, I will not, and more of his soldiership I don't know, except, in that country — England — he had the honor to be the officer at a place there called Mile End, to instruct for the doubling of files. I would do the man what honor I can, but of this — his service at Mile End — I am not certain."

The citizen militia of London used to train at Mile End Green, where they engaged in such military drills as the doubling of files. This was not a professional militia, and it was mocked for its amateurishness.

The first lord said, "He has out-villained villainy so far that the rarity redeems him. His villainy is so excessive that it is entertaining rather than simply despicable."

Bertram said, "I say a pox on him; he's still a cat."

The first lord was right: Parolles' insults were inventive and entertaining; in comparison, Bertram's insults were repetitive and boring.

The first soldier said to Parolles, "His qualities being at this poor price, I need not ask you if gold will corrupt him to revolt."

Parolles replied, "Sir, for a small French coin he will sell the fee-simple of his salvation, the inheritance of it, and cut the entail from all remainders, and a perpetual succession for it perpetually."

In other words, for a small French coin he would sell his eternal salvation, ensure that his immediate descendants would not inherit it, and furthermore ensure that *all* his descendants would not possess it.

"What kind of man is his brother, the other Captain Dumain?" the first soldier asked.

The second lord, who was the other Captain Dumain, asked, "Why does he ask him about me?"

"What kind of man is he?" the first soldier repeated.

"He is even a crow of the same nest," Parolles replied. "He is not altogether as great as the first in goodness, but greater a great deal in evil. He excels his brother as a coward, yet his brother is reputed one of the best cowards who exists. In a retreat he outruns any lackey who runs alongside his master's carriage; in contrast, when he is supposed to march forward to meet the enemy, his legs cramp."

The first soldier asked, "If your life is saved, will you undertake to betray the Duke of Florence?"

"Yes, and also the Captain of his cavalry, Count Rousillon," Parolles replied.

"I'll confer quietly with the General, and find out what he wants to do," the first soldier said.

Parolles said quietly to himself, "I'll have no more of military drumming — a plague on all military drums! I have run into this danger only because I wanted to seem to deserve well, and to beguile the supposition of that lascivious young boy, the Count Rousillon. Yet who would have suspected an ambush where I was captured?"

"There is no remedy, sir," the first soldier said. "You must die, the General says, you who have so traitorously revealed the secrets of your army and made such pestiferous reports of men with very noble reputations. You can serve the world for no honest use; therefore, you must die. Come, headsman, off with his head."

"Oh, Lord, sir! Let me live, or let me see my death!" Parolles pleaded. "At least, take off my blindfold."

The first lord said, "You shall have your blindfold taken off, and you shall take your leave of all your friends."

The first lord removed Parolles' blindfold and then asked him, "So, look around you. Do you know anybody here?"

"Good morning, noble Captain," Bertram said.

"God bless you, Captain Parolles," the second lord said.

"May God save you, noble Captain," the first lord said.

The second lord asked, "Captain, what greeting will you send to my Lord Lafeu? I am going to France and can take him your greeting."

The first lord asked, "Good Captain, will you give me a copy of the sonnet you wrote to Diana on behalf of the Count Rousillon? If I were not a complete coward, I would compel you to give it to me, but fare you well."

Bertram and the lords exited.

The first soldier said to Parolles, "You are ruined. You are undone, Captain, all but your scarf; that still has a knot in it."

"Who cannot be crushed by a plot?" Parolles said.

The first soldier said, "If you could find a country where there were only women who had received so much shame, you might begin an impudent, shameless nation. Fare you well, sir; I am going to France, too. We shall speak about you there."

The first soldier exited with the other soldiers.

Alone, Parolles said to himself, "Still I am thankful. If my heart were great, it would burst with shame at this. Captain I'll be no more, but I will eat and drink, and sleep as softly and gently as any Captain shall. Simply being the base thing I am shall make me live. That man who knows that he is a braggart, let him fear this, for it will come to pass that every braggart shall be found to be an ass. Rust, sword! Cool, blushes! And, Parolles, live safest in shame! Since you have been fooled, by Foolery thrive! There's a position and a means to live for every man alive."

If Parolles were a better man, he would die from shame. But he was not a better man, and he knew it, so he resolved to live and to eat, drink, and sleep well. Since he had been made a fool of, why not make a living by being a Fool?

Parolles did not know it, but the first lord had found his foolishness entertaining; others would as well.

Parolles then said before exiting, "I'll go after them."

Helena, the widow, and Diana spoke together in a room in the widow's house in Florence.

Helena said to the others, "That you may well perceive I have not wronged you, one of the greatest in the Christian world — the King of France — shall be my surety, aka guarantor, before whose throne it is needful, before I can fully accomplish my goals, to kneel.

"Previously, I did for him a desirable task, as dear almost as his life. Gratitude for this task would peep forth through the flinty bosom of a Tartar, one of a people not known in our society for gratitude, and would respond with thanks.

"I duly am informed that his grace the King is at Marseilles, to which place we have convenient and appropriate means of transportation. You must know that I am thought to be dead. Now that the army is disbanding, my husband is hurrying home, where with Heaven's aid and with the permission of my good lord the King, we'll be before we are expected."

The widow said, "Gentle madam, you have never had a servant to whose trust your business was more welcome. I am glad that you are able to confide in me."

Helena replied, "Nor have you, mistress, ever had a friend whose thoughts more truly labor to recompense your love and friendship. Doubt not that Heaven brought me up to provide your daughter's dowry for a good marriage, and doubt not that Heaven fated your daughter to be my motive — my means of causing my husband to act in a certain way — and helper to a husband.

"But, oh, strange men! They can make such sweet use of what they hate, when lecherous trusting of the deceived thoughts defiles the pitch-black night, and so lust plays with what it loathes — me, Helena — in place of that which is away and not present — Diana. His lust made him enjoy me, whom he hates.

"Bertram's lust that he trusted was deceived, and defiled the pitch-black night and made it even darker with his attempt to commit adultery, which he believed that he had committed although actually he slept with me and not with Diana.

"But let's talk further about this later.

"You, Diana, under my poor instructions yet must suffer to some extent on my behalf."

Diana replied, "As long as it is an honest, chaste death that goes with your impositions, I am willing to suffer death at your command."

Helena said, "Yet, I tell you this: With merely the word the time will bring on a metaphorical summer, when briers shall have leaves as well as thorns, and be as sweet as sharp."

"The word" is Bertram saying "yes" to his marriage vows — and meaning it. Once Bertram truly commits to his marriage vows, all will be well.

Helena continued, "We must leave. Our wagon is prepared, and time invigorates us. All's well that ends well; always the end crowns the work."

The Latin "*finis coronat opus*" means "the end crowns the work."

Helena continued, "Whatever the course, the end is the renown. Whatever occurs to get us there, the conclusion determines the praise."

The Countess, Lafeu, and the Fool spoke together in a room in the Count of Rousillon's palace. They were talking about Bertram and Parolles.

Lafeu said to the Countess, "No, no, no, your son was misled by a snipped-taffeta fellow there, whose villainous saffron would have made all the unbaked and doughy — raw — youth of a nation in his color."

A fashion of the time was to wear two sets of sleeves of different colors. The set of sleeves on the outside was made of taffeta and had cuts in them in order to reveal the color of the set of sleeves underneath. Parolles wore such fashionable clothing, some of which was saffron-colored, and Lafeu was saying that Parolles' influence on inexperienced young men would make them that color — saffron, aka yellow, symbolic color of cowardice.

Lafeu continued, "If not for Parolles, your daughter-in-law would have been alive at this hour, and your son would still be here at home, and more advanced in wealth and status by the King than by that red-tailed bumblebee I speak of."

Parolles was the red-tailed buzzing bumblebee; he wore fancy clothing and made noise as he chattered.

The Countess said, "I wish I had never known him; it resulted in the death of the most virtuous gentlewoman whom nature ever had praise for creating. If she had partaken of my flesh, and cost me the dearest groans of a mother in childbirth, I could not have owed her a more-rooted love. I loved Helena."

"She was a good lady," Lafeu said. "She was a good lady. We may pick a thousand salads before we light on such another herb."

The Fool said, "Indeed, sir, she was the sweet marjoram of the salad, or rather, the herb of grace."

The herb of grace is rue.

Lafeu said, "Marjoram and rue are knot-herbs. They are not for salads, you knave; they are nose-herbs. They are for smelling, not for eating."

Flowers and sweet-smelling herbs were grown in intricately designed beds called knots.

The Fool replied, "I am no great Nebuchadnezzar, sir; I have not much skill in either grace or grass."

Nebuchadnezzar, the King of Babylon, fell out of the grace of God, went insane, and ate grass like an animal. His story is told in the Biblical Book of Daniel.

"Which do you profess yourself to be: a knave or a fool?" Lafeu asked.

The Fool replied, "A Fool, sir, at a woman's service, and a knave at a man's."

"Why do you make this distinction?" Lafeu asked.

The Fool replied, "I would cheat the man of his wife and do his service."

"So you would be a knave at his service, indeed," Lafeu said.

"And I would give his wife my bauble, sir, to do her service," the Fool said.

He was punning. To service an animal is to mate it. A literal Fool's bauble is a scepter with the figure of a head on one end. The Fool was using the word "bauble" metaphorically to refer to his penis, which he would use to service a man's wife.

Lafeu replied, "I will answer my question for you: You are both a knave and a Fool."

"At your service," the Fool said.

"No, no, no," Lafeu said. The Fool already worked for the Countess. Lafeu liked the Countess, and he did not want to hire the Fool away from her.

"Why, sir, if I cannot serve you," the Fool said, "I can serve as great a Prince as you are."

"Who would that be?" Lafeu asked. "A Frenchman?"

"Truly, sir, he has an English name; but his fisnomy — physiognomy, aka facial features — is hotter in France than in England," the Fool said.

"What Prince is that?" Lafeu asked.

"The Black Prince, sir," the Fool said, "alias the Prince of Darkness, alias the Devil."

Edward the Black Prince was the son of King Edward III of England. He was called the Black Prince because of his black armor. In 1346, on a French battlefield, he played the role of a hero as he and his soldiers defeated the entire French army in the Battle of Crécy. He is why the Black Prince had an English name.

What was the Black Prince's French name? The Devil is associated with fire, as well as with blackness, and the French name "Lafeu" means "The Fire." The Fool was joking that Lafeu had the facial features of the Devil.

Lafeu appreciated the joke; he tipped the Fool.

He said, "Wait, there's some money for you. I am giving you this tip not to tempt you from your master you are talking about; continue to serve the Devil."

The Fool then claimed to be heading toward Heaven.

He said, "I am a woodland fellow, sir, who has always loved a great fire; and the master I speak about always keeps a good fire. But surely he is the Prince of the World; let his nobility remain in his court. I am for the house with the narrow gate, which I take to be too little for pomp to enter. Some people who humble themselves may enter, but the many will be too sensitive to cold and too fond of comfort, and they'll be for the flowery way that leads to the broad gate and the great fire."

"Go your ways and leave now," Lafeu said. "I begin to be weary of you, and I tell you that before I do in fact get weary of you, because I would not fall out with you. Go on your way: Let my horses be well looked after, without any tricks."

Some unethical hostlers were reputed to grease the horse's teeth with candlewax so that it could not eat many oats. Other hostlers were reputed to butter hay because horses will not eat buttered hay. That way, the hostler could charge horses' owners over and over for the same bundle of hay.

"If I put any tricks upon them, sir, they shall be jades' tricks," the Fool replied, "which are their own right by the law of nature."

Jades were ill-trained or bad horses, which had their own tricks. While being saddled by an inexperienced rider, a horse could fill its lungs with air. When the inexperienced rider attempted to climb onto the horse, the saddle would slide down to the horse's belly.

The Fool exited.

Lafeu said, "The Fool is a shrewd and unhappy knave."

Some people respond to their unhappy cynicism by creating humor; Lafeu thought that the Fool was one such person. Professional Fools create satire, and some satirists are unhappy cynics.

"So he is," the Countess said. "My lord and husband who has gone to Heaven got much entertainment out of him. By my husband's request and authority, the Fool remains here, and the Fool thinks my husband's authority gives him carte blanche to be saucy and impertinent. Indeed, the Fool has no pace, but runs where he will."

A trained horse keeps to a measured, steady pace, but the Fool was like a wild horse that ran wherever and however it wanted.

"I like him well," Lafeu admitted. "His sauciness is not amiss. I take no offence to it."

He added, "I was about to tell you that since I heard of the good lady's death and that my lord your son was returning home, I urged the King my master to speak on behalf of my daughter. His majesty, without being prompted, remembered by himself that when they were children, he had first proposed that they be married.

"His highness has promised me that he will arrange the marriage, and there is no better way to stop the displeasure he has conceived against your son. This marriage will reconcile the King and your son.

"How does your ladyship like it? Do you approve of your son marrying my daughter?"

"I am very much content, my lord," the Countess said, "and I wish it happily effected. I am happy for the marriage to take place."

"His highness comes posthaste from Marseilles," Lafeu said. "He is of as able body as when he was thirty years old. He will be here tomorrow, or I am deceived by a man who has seldom failed in gathering such information."

"This news makes me rejoice," the Countess said. "I have hoped that I shall see the King before I die. I have received letters telling me that my son will be here tonight. I ask your lordship to remain with me until my son and the King meet together."

"Madam, I was just thinking about what manners I might use to properly ask to be invited into your home for this meeting," Lafeu said.

"You need only plead the privilege that goes with your honored self," the Countess said. "As the father of the woman who will marry my son, you may certainly stay here."

"Lady, of that marriage I have made a bold charter, but I thank my God it holds yet," Lafeu said. "I boldly took action to make the marriage happen, and I am happy that it will happen."

The Fool returned and said, "Oh, madam, yonder's my lord your son with a patch of velvet on his face. Whether there is a scar under it or not, the velvet knows, but it is a splendid patch of velvet. His left cheek is a cheek of two pile and a half, but his right cheek is worn bare."

A velvet patch was used to cover a facial war wound. Velvet of two pile and a half was good-quality velvet.

Lafeu said, "A scar nobly got, or a noble scar, is a good livery — visible sign — of honor, so most likely that is why he is wearing the velvet."

The Fool said, "But it is your carbonadoed face."

Meat that has been carbonadoed for cooking has had slits made in it. The Fool was still thinking of fire, but he was also thinking of a different reason for wearing a velvet patch. A person with syphilitic sores on his face would have the sores slashed so that the infection could drain.

Lafeu said to the Countess, "Let us go see your son, please. I long to talk with the young noble soldier."

The Fool said, "Indeed, there's a dozen of them, with delicate fine hats and very courteous feathers that bow their heads and nod at every man."

CHAPTER 5

— 5.1 —

Helena, the widow, and Diana, accompanied by two attendants, stood on a street in Marseilles.

Helena said, "But this exceedingly great haste as we journey day and night must be wearing your spirits low. We cannot help it, but since you have made the days and nights as one and are wearing out your gentle limbs in my affairs, be certain that you so grow in my recompense that nothing can unroot you. You will be rewarded — you can be confident of that."

A gentleman walked down the street.

Seeing him, Helena said, "This is a good time to see a gentleman. This man may help me be heard by his majesty's ear, if he would expend some effort on my behalf."

She said to the gentleman, "May God save you, sir."

"And you," the gentleman replied.

"Sir, I have seen you in the court of the King of France," Helena said.

"I have been there sometimes," the gentleman replied.

"I do presume, sir, that you still have a reputation as a good man, and therefore, since I am goaded by many pressing reasons, which force me to put aside formal etiquette, I ask you for the use of your own virtues, for which I shall now and continue to be thankful to you."

"What do you want me to do?" the gentleman asked.

"I hope that you will please give this poor petition to the King of France and aid me with that store of power you have to come into the King's presence."

"The King's not here," the gentleman said.

"Not here, sir!" Helena exclaimed.

"Not here, indeed," the gentleman said. "He departed from here last night and with more haste than is his custom."

"Lord, how we lose our pains!" the widow said.

Unruffled, Helena said, "All's well that ends well yet, although time seems to us so adverse and our resources unfit."

She asked the gentleman, "Please tell us where he has gone."

"Indeed, as I understand it, he has gone to Rousillon, where I am going."

"Please, sir," Helena said, "since you are likely to see the King before I do, hand this paper to his gracious hand."

She gave him a paper.

Helena continued, "Your doing this I presume shall render to you no blame but rather make you thank your pains for doing it. I will follow you with what good speed our resources will contrive for us."

"I'll do this for you," the gentleman said.

"And you shall find yourself well thanked," Helena said, "no matter what happens. We must start traveling again. Go, go, help us."

The Fool and Parolles stood in front of the Count of Rousillon's palace.

Parolles, whose fortunes had drastically declined, and whose clothing was much less clean than formerly, asked the Fool very politely, "Good Monsieur Lavache, give my Lord Lafeu this letter. I have before now, sir, been better known to you, when I have held familiarity with fresher clothes, but I am now, sir, muddied because of Lady Fortune's moody dislike of me, and I smell somewhat strongly of her strong displeasure."

Parolles smelled as if he had fallen into a fishpond. In this society, garbage was thrown into ponds, where fish, including carp, were raised for food.

The Fool replied, "Truly, Lady Fortune's displeasure is only sluttish, if it smells as strongly as you speak of it. I will henceforth eat no fish of Lady Fortune's buttering. Please, stand downwind so that I don't smell you."

Fish were frequently buttered when served.

"You don't need to hold your nose, sir," Parolles said. "I was speaking metaphorically."

"Indeed, sir, if your metaphor stinks, I will hold my nose," the Fool said. "I would do that against any man's stinking metaphor. Please, stand further away."

Parolles requested, "Please, sir, deliver this paper to Lord Lafeu for me."

"Bah! Please stand further away," the Fool said. "You want me to give a paper from Lady Fortune's toilet to a nobleman! Look, here he comes himself."

Lafeu walked over to them.

The Fool said to him, "Here is a purr of Lady Fortune's, sir, or of Lady Fortune's cat — but not a musk-cat — who has fallen into the unclean fishpond of her displeasure, and, as he says, is muddied because of this. Please, sir, treat the carp as you may; for he looks like a poor, decayed, ingenious, foolish, rascally knave. I do pity his distress in my smiles of comfort and leave him to your lordship."

In this society, the word "purr" means many things: 1) the purr of a cat, 2) the knave in a deck of cards used to play the game Post and Pair, and 3) animal manure.

Civit cats and musk deer were known for their glands that were used to make perfume. Parolles' scent was nothing like the sweet-smelling scents of perfume.

Carp refers both to the fish and to a human chatterbox.

The Fool used "smiles of comfort" ironically. His smiles — jokes directed at Parolles' misfortune — hardly comforted Parolles. However, the Fool did call Parolles ingenious, which is a compliment. Although Parolles was a scoundrel, his scurrility was so thorough going that other people marveled at it and had a kind of respect for him.

The Fool exited.

Parolles said to Lafeu, "My lord, I am a man whom Lady Fortune has cruelly scratched."

"And what would you have me do about it?" Lafeu asked. "It is too late to pare her fingernails now. What have you done to play the knave with Lady Fortune, with the result being that she should scratch you? She in herself is a good lady and would not have knaves thrive long under her. There's a quart d'ecu — a small coin — for you. Let the justices make you and Lady Fortune friends. I am busy."

Some justices' jobs were to take care of the poor.

Parolles said, "I beg your honor to hear me say one single word more."

Lafeu said, "You are begging for a single penny more. Here, you shall have it. Don't bother speaking your word."

"My name, my good lord, is Parolles," he said.

Lafeu said, "You beg more than one 'word,' then," referring to Parolles' name. In French, the word "*paroles*" meant "words."

Looking closer at the bedraggled Parolles, and recognizing him, Lafeu said, "God's passion! Give me your hand. How is your drum?"

He had heard all about Parolles' adventure with the drum.

Parolles cried, "Oh, my good lord, you were the first who found me out and discovered what kind of a man I really am!"

"Was I, truly?" Lafeu said. "Then that means I was the first who lost you."

"It lies in you, my lord, to bring me in some grace, for you did bring me out," Parolles said.

"Get out, knave!" Lafeu said. "Do you put upon me at once both the duty of God and the duty of the Devil? One brings you in grace and the other brings you out of grace."

Trumpets sounded.

Lafeu said, "The King's coming; I can tell by his trumpets. Sirrah, ask for me later. I had a conversation about you last night. Although you are a fool and a knave, you shall eat; come on, follow me."

Parolles had fallen greatly in status, as shown by Lafeu calling him "sirrah." But Lafeu would provide for him: Lafeu would keep Parolles fed in return for Parolles' amusing him.

Parolles said, "I praise and thank God for you."

The King of France, the Countess, Lafeu, the two French lords, and some attendants were in a room in the Count of Rousillon's palace.

Using the royal plural, the King said to the Countess, "We lost a jewel when we lost Helena and our own worth and value were made much poorer by it, but your son, as if he were insane in his foolishness, lacked the sense to fully know her worth and value."

"That is in the past, my liege," the Countess said, "and I beg your majesty to consider that it was done because of natural rebellion. It was done in the blaze of youth, when oil and fire, too strong for reason's force, overbears it and burns on."

"Oil" means "semen," while "fire" is sexual desire. The Countess wanted the King to believe that her son's passions had opposed his reason, and to not believe that her son had opposed the King. Actually, it was Bertram's pride that had caused him to reject Helena because of her low birth. If he had been ruled by passion, he would have slept with her. However, it should be noted that the Countess meant that her son had felt passion for a woman other than Helena.

"My honored lady," the King replied, "I have forgiven and forgotten all; although my revenges were high bent like an arrow in a fully bent bow, and I watched for the best time to shoot him."

"This I must say," Lafeu said, "but first I beg for pardon. The young lord did to his majesty, his mother, and his lady offence of mighty note, but he did to himself the greatest wrong of all. He lost a wife whose beauty astonished the survey of the most experienced eyes, whose words took all ears captive, whose dear perfection made hearts that scorned to serve others humbly serve her."

"Praising what is lost makes the remembrance dear," the King said. "Well, call Bertram to come here. We and he are reconciled, and the first view of him shall kill all reopening of old wounds. Let him not ask for our pardon. The nature of his great offence is dead, and deeper than oblivion we bury its relics that would incense anger. We will not entertain any thoughts that arouse anger toward him. Let him approach me as if he were a stranger who had never offended me, and inform him that it is our will he should do this."

An attendant said, "I shall, my liege." He exited to carry out his errand.

The King asked Lafeu, "What does he say about your daughter? Have you spoken to him?"

"All that he is, is at the disposal of your highness," Lafeu replied.

"Then we shall have a match," the King said. "Bertram and your daughter will be married. I have letters that were sent to me that set him high in fame and reputation. He served well in war."

Bertram entered the room.

"He looks well after his experience in Italy," Lafeu said.

The King said, "I am not a day of a single season, for you may see a sunshine and a hail in me simultaneously, but to the brightest beams divided clouds give way, so come forward, Bertram. The time is fair again."

"For my faults, which I highly repent, dear sovereign, give pardon to me," Bertram said.

The King replied, "All is well and good. Say not one word more about the time that has passed by. Let's take the instant by the forelock, the way that we should seize Lady Fortune and opportunity, for we are old, and on our quickest decrees the inaudible and noiseless foot of Time steals before we can effect them. Do you remember the daughter of this lord: Lafeu?"

"Admiringly, my liege," Bertram said. "At first I struck my choice upon her, before my heart dared to make too bold a herald of my tongue."

Bertram was saying that he loved Lafeu's daughter first and wanted to marry her, but he was too shy to make his desire to marry her known.

He continued, this time speaking about Helena without mentioning her name, "The sight of Lafeu's daughter became implanted in my eyes, and contempt lent me a scornful perspective, which warped the line of every face other than the face of Lafeu's daughter and which scorned a fair color, or expressed that the fair color was stolen, and which extended or contracted all proportions to a most hideous object."

Bertram was saying that his love for Lafeu's daughter warped his perception of every other woman, including Helena, making him see Helena in a false light. The implication was that this caused him to reject marriage to Helena.

He continued talking about Helena: "Thence it came that she whom all men praised and whom I myself, since I have lost her, have loved, was in my eye the speck of dust that offended it."

In other words, before Helena died, the sight of her offended Bertram. But since Helena had died, he had come to love her.

"Well excused," the King said. "That you loved Helena strikes some bad deeds away from the great account of your good and bad deeds, but love that comes too late, like a remorseful pardon slowly carried, to the great sender becomes a sour offence, and love cries, 'She who is gone is good.'"

A pardon too slowly carried arrives too late to help the pardoned person, thus giving the pardoner a bad feeling. Love that comes too late is like that; Bertram said that he loved Helena, but he said that only after she had died, when he could only mourn her.

The King continued, "Our rash faults make a trivial valuation of important, serious things we have, not knowing them until we know their grave. Often our displeasures, which are to ourselves unjust, destroy our friends and afterward weep over their ashes and dust. Our own love waking cries to see what's done, while shame very late sleeps out the afternoon. Love comes to its senses too late, only after our displeasures have destroyed our friends.

"Let this be this sweet Helen's knell, and now forget her. Send forth your amorous token for fair Madeleine, Lafeu's daughter. The main consents are had, and here we'll stay to see our widower's second marriage-day."

The Countess said, "Make this marriage better than the first, dear Heaven. Bless it! Or, before my son and Lafeu's daughter meet, Nature, cease my existence!"

Lafeu said to Bertram, who was supposed to soon be his son-in-law, "Come on, my son, in whom my house's name must be digested — my daughter will take your name, while my house's name will be swallowed up — give a favor from you to sparkle in the spirits of my daughter, so that she may quickly come."

Bertram gave him a ring.

Lafeu looked at the ring and said, "By my old beard, and every hair that's on it, Helen, who is dead, was a sweet creature. Such a ring as this, the last time that I took her leave at court, I saw upon her finger."

He had kissed Helena's hand when he took leave of her, and so he had closely observed her ring.

"This ring was not hers," Bertram said. It was the ring that he thought that Diana had given to him.

"Now, please, let me see it," the King said. "My eye, while I was speaking, often was fastened on it."

He looked at the ring and said, "This ring was mine, and when I gave it to Helen, I told her that if her fortunes ever stood in necessity of help, if she sent this token to me I would relieve her. Do you have the craftiness to rob and deprive her of what should help her most?"

"My gracious sovereign," Bertram said, "however it pleases you to take it so, the ring was never hers."

The Countess said, "Son, I swear on my life, I have seen her wear it, and she valued it as much as she valued her life."

"I am sure I saw her wear it," Lafeu said.

"You are deceived, my lord; Helena never saw this ring," Bertram said. "While I was in Florence, this ring was thrown to me from a window. It was wrapped in a paper, which contained the name of the woman who threw it. She was a noblewoman, and she thought I was single, but when I had acknowledged that I was married and had informed her fully that I could not answer in that course of honor as she had made the overture, she was sad because of this knowledge and ceased pursuing me, although she would never take the ring back again."

As would soon become apparent, Bertram was lying.

The King said, "Plutus, the god of wealth himself, who knows the tincture and elixir that will turn base metals into gold, thus multiplying the precious metal, has not more knowledge of the mystery of Nature than I have knowledge of this ring. It was mine, and then it was Helen's. These things are true no matter who gave the ring to you. So then, if you have self-knowledge, confess that it was hers, and then confess by what rough enforcement you got this ring from her. She called on the saints to be her guarantors that she would never take this ring off her finger, unless she gave it to you yourself in bed, where you have never come to be with her, or if she sent it to us after she had suffered a great disaster."

"She never saw this ring," Bertram repeated.

"You lie," the King said. "As I love my honor, I swear that you lie. You make misgiving fears come to me that I would gladly shut out of my mind."

The King was afraid that Bertram had murdered Helena.

He continued, "If it should prove that you are so inhuman ... it will not prove to be true ... and yet I don't know that ... you hated her with a deadly hatred, and she is dead. Nothing, except to close her eyes myself, could make me believe that she is dead more than to see this ring. Take him away."

Guards seized Bertram.

The King said, "The evidence that was already in my possession before I acquired the evidence of this ring, however this matter turns out, shall accuse my fears of little foolishness and vanity, since I foolishly and vainly feared too little."

In other words, the evidence the King had previously acquired would show that the King's fears were not foolish and were not in vain, aka devoid of value; instead, the King had foolishly and vainly not feared enough.

He put the ring on his finger and ordered, "Take Bertram away! We'll examine this matter further."

Bertram said, "If you shall prove that this ring was ever hers, you shall as easily prove that I, as her husband, shared her bed in Florence, a city that Helena has never been in."

The guards took Bertram away.

The King said, "My thoughts are dismal."

The gentleman whom Helena had asked to deliver a paper to the King (see 5.1) entered the room and said, "Gracious sovereign, whether I have been to blame or not, I don't know. Here's a petition from a Florentine, who has for four or five of your stopping places on your journey arrived too late to deliver it to you yourself. I undertook to deliver this petition to you, vanquished by the fair grace and speech of the poor suppliant, who by this time I know is here in Rousillon waiting to talk to you. Her importuning appearance showed that her business is important, and she told me, in a sweet verbal summary, that her business did concern your highness with herself."

The King took the petition, which soon became apparent was from Diana and was about Bertram, and read it out loud:

"Upon his many protestations to marry me when his wife was dead, I blush to say it, he won me. I slept with him. Now that the Count Rousillon is a widower, his vows are legally due to me, and my honor is paid to him. He is legally obliged to marry me, but he stole away from Florence, taking no leave of me, and I have

"*DIANA CAPILET.*"

Hearing this, Lafeu immediately decided that he did not want Bertram to marry his daughter.

Lafeu said, "I will buy myself a son-in-law at a fair and pay the toll for this one. I'll have nothing to do with him."

Fairs were notorious for selling stolen goods, but Lafeu was saying that he could buy a better son-in-law than Bertram at a fair. He was also saying that he would pay the toll that was required to sell something — in this case, Bertram — at a fair.

The King said, "The Heavens have thought well of you, Lafeu, and so they have brought forth this discovery."

In this culture, a respectable woman would not travel alone, and the King knew that other people must have traveled with her.

He ordered, "Seek these petitioners. Go speedily and bring the Count back again."

Attendants exited to carry out the orders.

He said to the Countess, "I am afraid that the life of Helen, lady, was foully snatched."

The King thought that Helena had been murdered on Bertram's orders.

The Countess said, "Now may justice be done on the doers!"

Bertram, guarded, returned.

The King said to him, "I wonder that you still desire to marry, sir, since wives are monsters to you, and since you flee from them as soon as you swear to marry them."

The widow and Diana entered the room.

The King asked, "What woman is that?"

Diana replied, "I am, my lord, a wretched Florentine, descended from the ancient Capilet. I understand that you know my petition to you, and therefore you know to what extent I may be pitied."

The widow said, "I am her mother, sir, whose age and honor both suffer under this complaint we bring, and both shall cease without your remedy. Unless you make the Count of Rousillon marry my daughter, my aged self and my honor will die."

"Come here, Count," the King said. "Do you know these women?"

"My lord, I neither can nor will deny that I know them," Bertram said. "Do they charge me with anything else?"

"Why do you look so strangely upon your wife?" Diana asked.

"She's no wife of mine, my lord," Bertram said.

"If you shall marry, you give away this hand," she said, pointing to his hand, "and that is mine because it was pledged to me as part of the betrothal ceremony. You give away Heaven's vows, and those are mine. You give away myself, which is known to be mine. For I by vow am so embodied yours and so united to you that she who marries you must marry me. She will either marry both of us or marry neither of us."

Lafeu said to Bertram, "Your reputation comes up too short for my daughter. Your reputation is deficient, and you are no husband for her."

Bertram said, "My lord, this is a foolish, doting, and desperate creature, whom I have laughed with sometime. Let your highness lay a more noble thought upon my honor than to think that I would sink it here. You should think more highly of my honor than to think I would lower myself by marrying this woman."

"Sir, as concerns my thoughts, you will find them ill friends to you until your deeds make them your friends. I hope that your honor proves to be fairer than I think it is."

"My good lord," Diana said, "ask him upon his oath, if he thinks he did not take my virginity."

"What do you say to her?" the King asked Bertram.

"She's impudent, my lord, and she was a common gamester — prostitute — to soldiers in the military camp," Bertram replied.

"He does me wrong, my lord," Diana said. "If I were a common prostitute, he might have bought me at a common price. Do not believe him. Oh, behold this ring, whose high sentimental value as an heirloom and great material value as a ring lack an equal, yet for all that he gave it to a common prostitute of the camp, if I am one."

"He blushes, and he is hit," the Countess said. "Of six preceding ancestors, that ring, conferred by will and testament to the succeeding heir, has been owned and worn. This woman is his wife. That ring's a thousand proofs."

The King said, "I thought you said that you saw someone here in court who could be your witness."

"I did, my lord," Diana said, "but I am loath to produce so bad a witness. His name's Parolles."

"I saw the man today, if he is a man," Lafeu said.

"Find him, and bring him here," the King ordered.

An attendant exited to carry out the order.

"What about him?" Bertram asked. "He's considered to be a most perfidious slave, with all the stains and blemishes of the world censured and disparaged, whose disposition sickens when it speaks a truth. Am I either to be considered that or this on the basis of what is uttered by this man who will say anything?"

The King said, "She has your ring."

"I suppose so," Bertram said, reluctantly. "It is certain I liked her, and mounted her and had sex with her in the wanton way of youth. She knew to keep her distance and played hard to get and angled for me, maddening my sexual eagerness with her restraint, as all impediments in the course of sexual desire create more sexual desire, and in the end, her infinite cunning, with her commonplace charm, subdued me to the point I met her price. She got the ring, and I had that which any inferior man might have haggled for at a market."

Diana said, "I must be patient and calm. You, who have dismissed and turned away a very noble first wife, may justly give me less than you gave her. I yet say to you — since you lack virtue, I will lose a husband — ask for your ring, I will return it to you, and you give my ring to me again."

"I don't have it," Bertram said.

"What ring was yours, I ask you?" the King asked Diana.

"Sir, my ring was much like the ring on your finger," Diana replied.

"Do you know this ring?" the King asked. "This ring was his recently."

"And this is the ring 'I' gave to him in bed," Diana said.

The King asked, "The story that you threw the ring to him out of a window is false then?"

"I have spoken the truth," Diana said.

Parolles entered the room.

Bertram said, "My lord, I confess that the ring was hers."

The King replied, "You boggle — become alarmed — shrewdly. Every feather startles you."

By "shrewdly," the King meant "severely," but Bertram boggled shrewdly in another sense: He knew that Parolles could provide evidence to corroborate Diana's testimony and so he had admitted that the ring was hers.

The King asked Diana about Parolles, "Is this the man you spoke of?"

"Yes, my lord."

The King said to Parolles, "Tell me, sirrah, but tell me the truth, I order you. Don't fear the displeasure of your master, whom I'll keep from harming you if you tell the truth. What do you know about him and this woman here?"

Parolles replied, "So please your majesty, my master has been an honorable gentleman. He has had tricks in him, which gentlemen have.'

Parolles did not want to offend either Bertram or the King, so he wanted his comments to be understood in more ways than one.

"Honorable gentleman" could be understood positively, but given Bertram's actions we would not call him an honorable gentleman in a positive sense. However, he is honorable in that he is touchy and proud about his honor, and he is a gentleman in that he engages in the tricks that many men of his position in society engage in.

The King said, "Come, come, get to the point: Did he love this woman?"

"Truly, sir, he did love her, but how?" Parolles said.

"Please tell us how," the King said.

"He did love her, sir, as a gentleman loves a woman," Parolles said.

"A woman" is "a female commoner" as opposed to "a gentlewoman."

"How is that?" the King asked.

"He loved her, sir, and he loved her not," Parolles said.

Bertram had sex with a woman, but he did not want to marry the woman. His "love" for her was sexual, not romantic.

The King said, "You are a knave, and you are no knave. What an equivocal companion is this man! This fellow is evasive and quibbling and equivocating!"

"I am a poor man, and at your majesty's command," Parolles said.

Lafeu said, "He's a good drummer, my lord, but a bad orator. He makes a lot of noise, but little sense."

"Do you know that he promised to marry me?" Diana asked Parolles.

"Truly, I know more than I'll speak," Parolles said.

"Won't you speak all that you know?" the King asked.

"Yes, so please your majesty," Parolles said. "I did go between them, as I said, but more than that, he loved her. Indeed he was mad for her, and talked of Satan and of Limbo and of Furies and I don't know what. He was in torment because he loved her. Yet I had so much credit and such a good reputation with them at that time that I knew of their going to bed, and of other proposals, such as him promising her marriage, and things that would bring down bad things on me if I were to speak about them; therefore, I will not speak what I know."

"You have spoken all already, unless you can say that they are married," the King said, "but you are too subtle and devious in giving your evidence; therefore, stand aside."

The King then said to Diana, "This ring I have, you say, was yours?"

"Yes, my good lord."

"Where did you buy it? Or who gave it to you?"

"It was not given to me, nor did I buy it."

"Who lent it to you?"

"It was not lent to me either."

"Where did you find it, then?"

"I did not find it."

"If it were yours by none of all these ways," the King asked, "how could you give it to him?"

"I never gave it to him," Diana said.

Lafeu said, "This woman's an easy glove, my lord; she goes off and on at pleasure. She is easily changeable."

"This ring was mine," the King said. "I gave it to his first wife."

"It might be yours or hers, for anything I know," Diana said.

"Take her away," the irritated King said. "I do not like her now. Take her to prison, and take Bertram away."

He said to Diana, "Unless you tell me where you got this ring, you die within this hour."

"I'll never tell you," Diana said.

"Take her away," the King ordered.

"I'll make good on my story, my liege," Diana said. "I can bring forward a witness."

"I think now that you are some common prostitute," the King said.

"By Jove, I swear that if I ever sexually knew a man, it was you," Diana said.

In other words, she swore that she was a virgin.

"Why have you accused him all this while?" the King said.

"Because he is guilty, and he is not guilty," Diana said. "He 'knows' I am no maiden, and he'll swear to it; I'll swear I am a maiden, and he does not know it. Great King, I am no strumpet, I swear by my life. I am either a virgin maiden, or else I am this old man's wife."

She was referring to Lafeu.

"She abuses our ears with her words," the King said. "Take her to prison."

Diana said to the widow, her mother, "Good mother, fetch my witness."

She added, "Wait, royal sir."

The widow exited.

Diana continued, "The jeweler who owns the ring is sent for, and 'he' shall be a witness for me. But as for this lord, who has abused me, as he 'knows' himself, although yet he never harmed me, here I quit — acquit and leave — him. He himself 'knows' he has defiled my bed. At that time he got his wife with child. Although she is 'dead,' she feels her young one kick. So there's my riddle: One who is 'dead' is quick — she is alive and she feels her unborn baby kicking."

The widow returned with Helena.

Diana continued, "And now behold the answer of the riddle."

The King asked, "Isn't there a magician present who beguiles the accurate function of my eyes and makes me see something that is not there? Is what I see real?"

Magicians were reputed to be able to raise the spirits of the dead.

"No, what you see is not real, my good lord," Helena said. "It is but the shadow of a wife you see, the name and not the thing."

Helena meant she had the title of "wife," but she was not a real wife because her husband had rejected her. But Bertram, seeing her and realizing from what had been said that he had slept with her and that she was pregnant with his child, immediately repented and immediately considered her to be his wife both in name and in deed.

He said to Helena, "You are both, both. I beg you to pardon and forgive me!"

"Oh, my good lord," Helena replied, "when you thought I was this maiden Diana, I found you wondrously kind. There is your ring, and look, here's your letter, which says this: '*When from my finger you can get this ring and are by me with child*,' et cetera. What the letter states as conditions have been done. Will you be mine, now you are doubly won?"

Bertram said to the King, "If she, my liege, can make me know clearly all that has happened, I'll love her dearly, ever, ever dearly."

Helena said, "If it does not appear plain and if it proves to be untrue, then may divorcing death step between me and you!"

She then said to the Countess, "Oh, my dear mother, do I see you living?"

Lafeu said, "My eyes smell onions; I shall weep soon."

He said to Parolles, "Good Tom Drum, lend me a handkerchief. So, I thank you. You shall go home with me and wait on me as a servant. I'll be entertained by you."

Parolles bowed obsequiously.

Lafeu said, "Let your courtesies alone, for they are scurvy ones. Stop bowing."

The King said, "Let us from point to point every particular point of this story know, to make the exact truth in pleasure flow."

He said to Diana, "If you are yet a fresh uncropped flower, choose for yourself a husband, and I'll pay your dower. For I can guess that by your honest aid, you kept a wife a wife, and you kept yourself a virgin maiden. Of that and all the progression of events, more or less, the resolution of loose ends more leisure shall express. All yet seems well, and if it ends the bitter past so fittingly and meet, then more welcome is the sweet."

EPILOGUE

The King now says to you, the reader:

"The King's a beggar, now the play is done.

"All is well ended, if this suit is won,

"That you express content, which we will repay,

"With striving to please you, day exceeding day.

"Ours be your patience then, and yours our parts;

"Your gentle hands lend us, and take our hearts."

In other words, the King and all the other characters in this book are actors, and they have been playing roles and striving more and more each day in order to entertain you, the readers, who are their audience. Now the "King" is a beggar who begs you for applause (and good reviews online). The "King" wants the audience and the actors to exchange roles. The audience can act by applauding while the actors make no more sounds, but the actors and playwright and book author will repay the applause (and good online reviews) with gratitude.

APPENDIX A: ABOUT THE AUTHOR

It was a dark and stormy night. Suddenly a cry rang out, and on a hot summer night in 1954, Josephine, wife of Carl Bruce, gave birth to a boy — me. Unfortunately, this young married couple allowed Reuben Saturday, Josephine's brother, to name their first-born. Reuben, aka "The Joker," decided that Bruce was a nice name, so he decided to name me Bruce Bruce. I have gone by my middle name — David — ever since.

Being named Bruce David Bruce hasn't been all bad. Bank tellers remember me very quickly, so I don't often have to show an ID. It can be fun in charades, also. When I was a counselor as a teenager at Camp Echoing Hills in Warsaw, Ohio, a fellow counselor gave the signs for "sounds like" and "two words," then she pointed to a bruise on her leg twice. Bruise Bruise? Oh yeah, Bruce Bruce is the answer!

Uncle Reuben, by the way, gave me a haircut when I was in kindergarten. He cut my hair short and shaved a small bald spot on the back of my head. My mother wouldn't let me go to school until the bald spot grew out again.

Of all my brothers and sisters (six in all), I am the only transplant to Athens, Ohio. I was born in Newark, Ohio, and have lived all around Southeastern Ohio. However, I moved to Athens to go to Ohio University and have never left.

At Ohio U, I never could make up my mind whether to major in English or Philosophy, so I got a bachelor's degree with a double major in both areas, then I added a master's degree in English and a master's degree in Philosophy.

Currently, and for a long time to come (I eat fruits and veggies), I am spending my retirement writing books such as *Nadia Comaneci: Perfect 10*, *The Funniest People in Dance*, *Homer's* Iliad: *A Retelling in Prose*, and *William Shakespeare's* Othello: *A Retelling in Prose*.

By the way, my sister Brenda Kennedy writes romances such as *A New Beginning* and *Shattered Dreams*.

APPENDIX B: SOME BOOKS BY DAVID BRUCE

Retellings of a Classic Work of Literature

Arden of Faversham: A Retelling

Ben Jonson's The Alchemist: *A Retelling*

Ben Jonson's The Arraignment, or Poetaster: *A Retelling*

Ben Jonson's Bartholomew Fair: *A Retelling*

Ben Jonson's The Case is Altered: *A Retelling*

Ben Jonson's Catiline's Conspiracy: *A Retelling*

Ben Jonson's The Devil is an Ass: *A Retelling*

Ben Jonson's Epicene: *A Retelling*

Ben Jonson's Every Man in His Humor: *A Retelling*

Ben Jonson's Every Man Out of His Humor: *A Retelling*

Ben Jonson's The Fountain of Self-Love, or Cynthia's Revels: *A Retelling*

Ben Jonson's The Magnetic Lady, or Humors Reconciled: *A Retelling*

Ben Jonson's The New Inn, or The Light Heart: *A Retelling*

Ben Jonson's Sejanus' Fall: *A Retelling*

Ben Jonson's The Staple of News: *A Retelling*

Ben Jonson's A Tale of a Tub: *A Retelling*

Ben Jonson's Volpone, or the Fox: *A Retelling*

Christopher Marlowe's Complete Plays: Retellings

Christopher Marlowe's Dido, Queen of Carthage: *A Retelling*

Christopher Marlowe's Doctor Faustus: *Retellings of the 1604 A-Text and of the 1616 B-Text*

Christopher Marlowe's Edward II: *A Retelling*

Christopher Marlowe's The Massacre at Paris: *A Retelling*

Christopher Marlowe's The Rich Jew of Malta: *A Retelling*

Christopher Marlowe's Tamburlaine, Parts 1 and 2: *Retellings*

Dante's Divine Comedy: *A Retelling in Prose*

Dante's Inferno: *A Retelling in Prose*

Dante's Purgatory: *A Retelling in Prose*

Dante's Paradise: *A Retelling in Prose*

The Famous Victories of Henry V: *A Retelling*

From the Iliad *to the* Odyssey: *A Retelling in Prose of Quintus of Smyrna's* Posthomerica

George Chapman, Ben Jonson, and John Marston's Eastward Ho! *A Retelling*

George Peele's The Arraignment of Paris: *A Retelling*

George Peele's The Battle of Alcazar: *A Retelling*

George Peele's David and Bathsheba, and the Tragedy of Absalom: *A Retelling*

George Peele's Edward I: *A Retelling*

George Peele's The Old Wives' Tale: *A Retelling*

George-a-Greene: *A Retelling*

The History of King Leir: *A Retelling*

Homer's Iliad: *A Retelling in Prose*

Homer's Odyssey: *A Retelling in Prose*

J.W. Gent.'s The Valiant Scot: *A Retelling*

Jason and the Argonauts: A Retelling in Prose of Apollonius of Rhodes' Argonautica

John Ford: Eight Plays Translated into Modern English

John Ford's The Broken Heart: *A Retelling*

John Ford's The Fancies, Chaste and Noble: *A Retelling*

John Ford's The Lady's Trial: *A Retelling*

John Ford's The Lover's Melancholy: *A Retelling*

John Ford's Love's Sacrifice: *A Retelling*

John Ford's Perkin Warbeck: *A Retelling*

John Ford's The Queen: *A Retelling*

John Ford's 'Tis Pity She's a Whore: *A Retelling*

John Lyly's Campaspe: *A Retelling*

John Lyly's Endymion, The Man in the Moon: *A Retelling*

John Lyly's Galatea: *A Retelling*

John Lyly's Love's Metamorphosis: *A Retelling*

John Lyly's Midas: *A Retelling*

John Lyly's Mother Bombie: *A Retelling*

John Lyly's Sappho and Phao: *A Retelling*

John Lyly's The Woman in the Moon: *A Retelling*

John Webster's The White Devil: *A Retelling*

King Edward III: *A Retelling*

Mankind: *A Medieval Morality Play* (A Retelling)

Margaret Cavendish's The Unnatural Tragedy: *A Retelling*

The Merry Devil of Edmonton: *A Retelling*

The Summoning of Everyman: *A Medieval Morality Play* (A Retelling)

Robert Greene's Friar Bacon and Friar Bungay: *A Retelling*

The Taming of a Shrew: *A Retelling*

Tarlton's Jests: A Retelling

Thomas Middleton's A Chaste Maid in Cheapside: *A Retelling*

Thomas Middleton's Women Beware Women: *A Retelling*

Thomas Middleton and Thomas Dekker's The Roaring Girl: *A Retelling*

Thomas Middleton and William Rowley's The Changeling: *A Retelling*

The Trojan War and Its Aftermath: Four Ancient Epic Poems

Virgil's Aeneid: *A Retelling in Prose*

William Shakespeare's 5 Late Romances: Retellings in Prose

William Shakespeare's 10 Histories: Retellings in Prose

William Shakespeare's 11 Tragedies: Retellings in Prose

William Shakespeare's 12 Comedies: Retellings in Prose

William Shakespeare's 38 Plays: Retellings in Prose

William Shakespeare's 1 Henry IV, aka Henry IV, Part 1: A Retelling in Prose

William Shakespeare's 2 Henry IV, aka Henry IV, Part 2: A Retelling in Prose

William Shakespeare's 1 Henry VI, aka Henry VI, Part 1: A Retelling in Prose

William Shakespeare's 2 Henry VI, aka Henry VI, Part 2: A Retelling in Prose

William Shakespeare's 3 Henry VI, aka Henry VI, Part 3: A Retelling in Prose

William Shakespeare's All's Well that Ends Well: A Retelling in Prose

William Shakespeare's Antony and Cleopatra: A Retelling in Prose

William Shakespeare's As You Like It: A Retelling in Prose

William Shakespeare's The Comedy of Errors: A Retelling in Prose

William Shakespeare's Coriolanus: A Retelling in Prose

William Shakespeare's Cymbeline: A Retelling in Prose

William Shakespeare's Hamlet: A Retelling in Prose

William Shakespeare's Henry V: A Retelling in Prose

William Shakespeare's Henry VIII: A Retelling in Prose

William Shakespeare's Julius Caesar: A Retelling in Prose

William Shakespeare's King John: A Retelling in Prose

William Shakespeare's King Lear: A Retelling in Prose

William Shakespeare's Love's Labor's Lost: A Retelling in Prose

William Shakespeare's Macbeth: A Retelling in Prose

William Shakespeare's Measure for Measure: A Retelling in Prose

William Shakespeare's The Merchant of Venice: A Retelling in Prose

William Shakespeare's The Merry Wives of Windsor: A Retelling in Prose

William Shakespeare's A Midsummer Night's Dream: A Retelling in Prose

William Shakespeare's Much Ado About Nothing: A Retelling in Prose

William Shakespeare's Othello: A Retelling in Prose

William Shakespeare's Pericles, Prince of Tyre: A Retelling in Prose

William Shakespeare's Richard II: A Retelling in Prose

William Shakespeare's Richard III: A Retelling in Prose

William Shakespeare's Romeo and Juliet: A Retelling in Prose

William Shakespeare's The Taming of the Shrew: A Retelling in Prose

William Shakespeare's The Tempest: A Retelling in Prose

William Shakespeare's Timon of Athens: A Retelling in Prose

William Shakespeare's Titus Andronicus: A Retelling in Prose

William Shakespeare's Troilus and Cressida: A Retelling in Prose

William Shakespeare's Twelfth Night: A Retelling in Prose

William Shakespeare's The Two Gentlemen of Verona: A Retelling in Prose

William Shakespeare's The Two Noble Kinsmen: A Retelling in Prose

William Shakespeare's The Winter's Tale: A Retelling in Prose

www.ingramcontent.com/pod-product-compliance
Lightning Source LLC
Chambersburg PA
CBHW051839130726
47987CB00002B/614